Wild Hare

WHO Chains YOU PUBLISHING

LAURA KOERBER

Published by Who Chains You Publishing
P.O. Box 581
Amissville, VA 20106

www.WhoChainsYou.com

Book cover and interior design by Tamira Thayne

ISBN-13: 978-1-946044-51-8

Printed in the United States of America

First Edition

to my sister, with love

Author Disclaimer: This text refers to Raven, Coyote, and Wild Hare, all figures from Native American story telling and spirituality. The hares, coyotes and raven depicted in this novel do not correspond to the figures in Native spirituality. To really understand Wild Hare, Coyote, and Raven, please consult texts written from within Native culture. Raven is a Northwest coastal character, Coyote is more associated with the Southwest, and Wild Hare is from the Ojibwe tradition. My hares, coyotes, and ravens are more akin to the European tradition of fairies merged with the idea of nature spirits.

CHAPTER ONE

Monday Morning

"**T**he world is coming to an end, but my personal life is okay, I guess."

That was my response to Arne's "How're ya?" greeting. I pushed the oil rags and cigarette butts off the seat of his old pickup truck and climbed in. Arne is used to sour comments from me, so he just threw the truck into gear, gunned the engine, and smirked, "Someone's got a bee up his butt this morning."

I let a half mile of clear cut rumble past the window while I thought about my shitty mood. Arne was right; my mood was even shittier than normal. The low-hanging, pinkish-gray smoke from a distant forest fire was getting on my nerves in a quietly grinding way, like bad music or the smell of diesel oil: the kind of irritation that puts you in a crappy mood without you noticing how you got there.

We bounced down Highway 3, dodging potholes, while I contemplated the butchered landscape and wondered grimly if we were going to be on fire right there in Chippewa County soon. I didn't need a weather report to know it was unusually hot, even for late August. The whole summer had been hot and dry.

Back when I was a kid, I used to enjoy the ride to town

because of the way the road wound through a mosaic of wetlands and forest and lakes. There used to be lots of moose back then too: big, somber, stupid animals. I'd kind of admired the moose because they were so much better at parenting than my folks had ever been.

Mostly gone now: the forest, the marshes around the lakes, the moose.

Some of the clear-cut patches have grown back as stands of skinny pines and firs packed together like toothpicks in a box—not a real forest because the animals can't live in it. Not even a memory of a real forest. The ugly fake forest outside the truck windows pissed me off as much as the smoke. Every fucking thing was reminding me how fucked we all were. Then Arne asked, "What's the point of being a fucking fairy if you can't just wave a magic wand and get shit done?"

Yeah, I'm a fairy. No, not that kind. I'm half-human, half-forest spirit from the wild hare clan. There used to be lots of us, but most of the full fairies have either died or moved away with the death of the forest.

I kind of take care of Arne. That's the price I pay for enthralling him back when we were kids. He's a skinny, ratty-looking guy with no teeth and a face crevassed with wrinkles. He looks like life backed a pickup truck over him two or three times. He's my buddy, but I've never been good at saving him from his own bad judgment. Well, the truth is he's an alcoholic. And he's never been able to think more than a few days ahead.

It was Monday, and we were driving into town so I could help him go shopping. Sort of shopping. Arne needed to get some real roofing materials to replace the tarp on his trailer because he didn't want to go through another winter of leaks. He couldn't afford the sealant, which is why I was going to help him shop. That roofing stuff is basically tar. It's a stinky job putting that crap on, a job he didn't want to do because his back hurts all the time. So he wanted me to help him with the work as well as help him with the cost, which is what brings me back to his question: Why couldn't I use magic to get shit done for us? Like fix the roof or fix a car.

But Arne knows the answer, so I didn't say anything. He was just expressing his bad mood in his own way.

Besides I got distracted by the radio: jingle-jangle music and a lady's voice cheerfully singing something about "making our own happiness." I thought she was talking about growing your own weed—which I do and have been doing for years and, yeah, it makes me happy—but she went warbling on, and I realized that it was one of those government things like "President's Hour" and "Fly the Flag" events. An announcer burst into speech, "As America prepares for 'Make Your Own Happiness Month of 2032,' cities and towns everywhere are planning events to celebrate local business leaders who are creating wealth and employment through free enterprise . . ."

Arne cut her off. "Fucking bitch oughta give me something to be happy about," he muttered around his cigarette. I just looked out the window. I hadn't been a happy kid, and I'd been a stupid, angry young man, but that was because of family stuff: I got in trouble a lot due to being half-fairy with a schizophrenic father and a mother who'd been invisible most of the time. I went through a lot of hassle at school and later with jobs until I got good at conning people and became a successful small time criminal.

So my personal life was pretty good. I owned one of the last stretches of virgin woods in northern Wisconsin, I had good friends, I had enough to eat, and I had no trouble getting sex when I really wanted it. I had the makings of happiness, if all I cared about was myself. But I didn't just care about myself, so I had this slow burn in my stomach all the time and hearing that smug asshole on the radio really made it flame up. I switched the radio off. "Why do you listen to that shit?" I asked.

"Fucking government." Arne grumbled, not answering my question. Arne doesn't have much happiness in his personal life. I think he listens to the radio so he can have something outside of his own life to be mad about.

We left the clear-cuts behind, and the "Report Illegal Aliens" sign hove into view—a huge billboard with a picture of a swarthy guy holding a gun, his wife next to him wrapped in black from head to foot—followed by the outskirts of Bear Lake. Arne stomped on the brakes because he had unpaid speeding tickets. They put people in jail now if they don't pay their fines, and then they charge you room and board so if you can't pay, you stay.

We slowed to a crawl past the gun shop and shooting range, rolled by the gas station and the diner, and then the highway morphed into Main Street. It's a good idea to drive slow through Bear Lake, even if you aren't scared of a fine, unless you *want* to kill someone. Summer people stroll out into traffic like zombies. Rich, some of them, but they don't spend much money in town. They just wander around getting in the way. Arne aimed at a potbellied bastard in golfing clothes but swerved at the last minute.

There's only three blocks of stores followed by the militia building, the city hall, and the county courthouse. After that, the town disintegrates into little houses, trailers, the hardware store, and the defunct sawmill. Bear Lake's the county seat, but it's a county that's losing human population. We stopped at the hardware store and climbed

4

down out of Arne's truck. I stretched; my back gets cramped up in that small space. Arne shambled into the store.

The hardware store is in a building from the fifties: one-story, blocky, with big front windows. Never an attractive building, it now looks frail and shabby. The interior is a dark and dusty hole full of shit in such a jumble that you'd need to be an archeologist to find what you want. They stay in business because they sell absolutely everything from birthday balloons to car tires; it's all in there somewhere.

The old guy who runs the place is blind, so I usually don't have to use glamour; I just straight up steal stuff from him. I sauntered in after Arne and peered around in the darkness. I had to dodge those flypaper strips full of dead flies hanging around everywhere. Gave the place a horror show atmosphere.

That old hardware store is one of the few businesses still holding on in Bear Lake. The old mom and pop resorts on the lakes in the area couldn't make money, so they sold out a few at a time. Some are condos now or timeshares or just private vacation houses. With the drop in seasonal tourists, there's a lot fewer people spending money in town to support the local businesses.

There's a mine about thirty miles away up near what used to be a national park. It's still a park officially, but the public and the fairies don't go there anymore; it's all torn up now. Polluted. The miners make some money, not real good but better than the minimum wage, but they live too far away to spend anything in Bear Lake unless they happen to come over for the fishing here—which some of them do, having fucked up the waters over where they live.

The point is the miners and the rich people aren't enough to keep the town going, which is fine with me when I get in a fuck-all-humans mood but hard on local businesses.

While I was thinking those grumpy thoughts, Arne found a clerk. I could see them in the dimness of the interior. The clerk was a stocky, box-shaped young man, probably trying to support a wife and a kid off the store's thin profits. He had the look of someone bearing bad news. I watched Arne flap his toothless mouth in dismay, probably at the price. The young man disappeared into the back and, sure enough, Arne lurched my way, bitching about costs, "Eighty-six fucking bucks. Can you believe it?"

We moved down toward the cash register. The old man stands there behind the counter all day long, but he never rings anything up. He just smiles at the air in front of his face. Since he can't recognize faces, he's friendly to everyone—at least until he figures out who he's talking to. Then sometimes he stops smiling.

Arne complained, "How come that sealer costs so much? Is the stuff made out of black gold?"

"Roof sealer?" The old man came to life. Having spent his whole existence studying hardware and building materials, he can talk about it like an evangelist on a tear about the Bible. "That stuff is acrylic-based and made from elastomeric silicone and will see you out. If you put it on right, you won't have to do it again, ever. Goes on to stay. Make sure you got a stretch of good weather ahead of you. It won't do to put it on if it's going to rain or even sprinkle, so check your weather report."

Arne just stared at him, stunned. We heard clumping and thumping and saw the thick young man briskly shoving a hand truck down the aisle, the can of sealer on board. I wondered if Arne needed more stuff—brushes? I'd done lots of repair crap around people's homes with Arne but hadn't sealed a trailer roof against leaks. The young guy set the hand truck down with a thunk and squeezed behind the counter.

"'Scuse me, Dad." His fingers hammered the old cash register. "That's eighty-six dollars and six forty-four more for the governor." Sales taxes are high even though the legislature never spends money on anything except trips for politicians and parties and statues. We got a statue of the governor last year. It's in front of the county building. Arne reached for his wallet.

That's when I made my move. I touched Arne on the arm to signal him to be quiet, and then I spoke calmly and firmly, looking straight into the young man's eyes. I said, "Arne already paid. He paid yesterday. You just forgot, but now you remember."

Suddenly the old guy started babbling again, "I know you. You never buy nothing. I hear you walking around, and then you walk out, and you never buy nothing." He was getting agitated. His son patted him on the back.

"It's okay, Dad," he laughed. "I forgot. They already paid. Here, let me run it out for you."

Arne smirked a secret grin at me. We followed the young man out, and the three of us stood around for a minute, each hoping that someone else would heave the damn can into the truck. In the end, we all grabbed it and hoisted it up onto the truck bed. It rolled with a heavy clunk up against the cab.

Arne said, "I still don't get why you can't just make it lift itself." The young guy gave him a what's-he-mean look, but I just stalked off and climbed into the cab. Arne joined me and snapped the radio on. Three country songs later we were out of town, past all the clear-cuts and old burns, and approaching the turn-off to the logging road that leads up to where Arne squats. That's when the jingle-jangle lady started chirping again about "Make Your Own Happiness", and I nearly yanked the knob off the radio getting it turned off.

"Hey," Arne complained, "Careful! What's with you anyway?" He glanced at me warily. "What are you so pissed off about?"

I didn't answer because I really didn't know. We'd just scored some free roofing materials. Arne was going to have a dry winter. I was on my way home. So why didn't I feel happy? Instead, I felt in some way that the burn in my stomach was spreading to my heart.

Looking back, I can see that's how it all started. The good stuff and the shitty stuff we went through that year began with that fucking "Make Your Own Happiness" crap. Because that year, the year we were all supposed to make our own happiness, was the year I went out and made mine. I made it the wrong way, and then I made it the right way, but I never made it the way the assholes wanted me to. I did it my own fucking way.

CHAPTER TWO:

Still Monday

After helping Arne hoist his can of sealant out of the truck, I climbed into my car and drove home. I live about five miles south of Arne, down the highway. There's a turn off the pavement onto a gravel road marked by a small sign that reads "Secret Lake."

The woods around the turnoff are about twenty years old—second growth timber owned by a timber company. Not a real forest. But there's a place a little ways up our road where suddenly everything changes because it's my land—a real forest—and the trees are huge and old. It's like driving into a cathedral. We've got sugar maple, yellow birch, white pine, white spruce, and white cedar with some balsam fir scattered around, plus sisterhoods of aspen along the meadows.

The trees were big when I was born because this forest has never been cut. My mother saw to that—she'd been the protector for many, many years before she married my dad and before I was born. And the trees are even bigger now: straight-trunked, heavy, ominous, wise old trees that have been watching, watching, watching for over two hundred years. Some are even older than that. They stand at intervals, giving each other space, respectful. Between them, the little maples and honeysuckles crowd together, happy in the shade. The effect is of greenness: filtered green light, layers of green leaves, and reflections of green thrown from the glowing leaves. I always get a little green myself and have to concentrate on staying in the human part of me.

I slowed down where the road goes from gravel to pine needles, just two ruts. In the summer it's easy to drive on, soft and gentle. Winters—well, sometimes we get stuck. My little sedan ground up an incline, wound around a bend, and suddenly I could see the lake.

It's one of those tea-colored lakes, golden brown from tree tannins. If you stare down into the water, the depths are full of golden light and shades of brown. The colors on the surface are always changing. Right then, as I looked out over the lake, the waters were white from the reflection of the fat, cumulous clouds, smeared with a pinkish gray from the smoke, and mixed with dark blue: the ripples of a playful wind. Along the far side, the water was a deep dark green, the color of wet pine needles.

It isn't a big lake, not like Lake Bear, which is big enough for water skiers. Our lake is just ten acres or so with marsh down at the far end where the creek exits and slides off downhill. Not round. It's more of a fat "C" shape, and there's a floating island full of ferns and willows and wildflowers. There're even some trout lilies on the island. You can't stand on the island because your feet will go right through, and the water's full of leeches. They're spectacular leeches, though, I'll give 'em that. About eight inches long and green with red spots. Scare the hell out of the tourists.

Tree-covered hills are the backdrop for the lake: steep-sided, low, and rounded. Our stream originates up there in an outbreak of rocks. This is country shaped by glaciers.

10

Some of the landscape is scraped flat down to the Canadian Shield, but mostly it's hills that formed ahead of the glacier like piles of snow in front of a snow plow. It's an ancient landscape that makes me feel both very old and very young. And very, very aware of time.

I pulled my old sedan up behind my cabin and got out. Didn't see Sally, Charlie, or Danni right off, but I heard the sound of someone chopping wood. I did see two tourists.

I own Secret Lake Resort, but Sally runs the place with Charlie, and Danni lived mostly in the lake. We have just six cabins: one for me and one for Sally and Charlie, leaving four to rent out. The cabins look like wooden boxes, mossy and decaying. Each has one big room with a little bitty kitchen on one side and a tiny bathroom and a covered porch that faces the lake.

There are canoes down by the water. We get fishermen pretty regular. Hunters don't come here much because, when they do, we make sure they don't bag anything. We also get the occasional oddball who has a desire for aloneness and *wants* to vacation in a funky resort at the ass end of nowhere.

Charlie was one of those. He came for the isolation but fit in with us real well. Sally offered him some cake, and that did it. He wasn't leaving after that. She gave him the cake because in his heart he wanted to stay, but his head told him no. Besides, she wanted a handyman to supplement me. He used to be a college professor, but now he's much happier.

There's usually no one at the lake but us. To my surprise that day, the day I drove up in a cranky and gloomy mood, I had neighbors.

I could tell everything about them right off because I'm a good judge of humans—we have to be; wild hares know all about the wolves. These two were poor and defiant about it. He had a thin, faded sports logo T-shirt over his gut, and she was pregnant.

That meant life was over for them. Their choices had narrowed down to which bill they were going to pay and which they were going to put off, a life of never getting ahead: rent, car repairs, babysitters when Grandma couldn't look after the kid, clothes for the kid, missed work because of the kid, Christmas for the kid. A relentless rat race that they would steadily lose as each year's mishaps were paid for by charge card, and debt piled up to unpayable levels.

So these two had decided to take their already over-loaded charge card and go on vacation somewhere cheap. And the prospective father was already well on his way to getting drunk. I decided to avoid them.

I cut around behind their cabin and headed for S, C, and D down at the end. I'd known Danni forever, but Sally had only been out at the resort for about five years. Sally is half raven clan from out by Washington state somewhere. Got a voice like the air brakes on a semi. Danni was a full water fairy. Her real name came from the Ojibwa language, but we called her "Danni" for short. A lot of the real fairies around here speak the language of the Ojibwa from long ago. Supposedly hundreds of years ago the Ojibwa and the fairies talked to each other all the time. Not any more, at least to my knowledge.

Anyway, since Sally and I are mixes, we live mostly like regular humans. Since Danni was the real thing, she lived in water and the forest, so most of the time we didn't see her. Charlie's just human, but he knows about us.

So I went looking for everyone and, when I rounded the corner to S and C's cabin, Sally was there with Charlie, but Danni was not present, at least not visibly. Charlie was chopping wood, and Sally was whacking a quilt with a broom. Clouds of dust hovered over them, mixed with mosquitoes and deer flies.

Sally looks to be in her thirties but really's a lot older. She's dark-haired, angular, and has bright beady eyes. Charlie's in his fifties and was a wimp when he first came out here, but he's gained a lot of muscle mass since he ate that cake. He's still kind of a stringy guy, but the dazed poetry professor air is gone. He now looks dazed and poetic in a more backwoods way—his thin dishwater hair is down to his shoulders, and his skin is burned to a permanent tannin color.

He dropped the ax and looked up as I came around the corner, wiping his arm across his forehead. Sally gave her quilt a final whack and called out, "Hey, brother!" I lifted one hand in a tired wave, slouched onto the porch, and collapsed into the Adirondack chair.

They gathered with me on the porch, Charlie perched on the railing and Sally in the other chair. Sally's porch is like the interior of her cabin and possibly the interior of her mind: cluttered with shiny bits of creativity. The colorful plastic toy unicorns that prance along the porch railing are hers. She has dream catchers everywhere, the more spidery and bead-bedecked the better. And she makes images out of pieces of old metal that she cuts crudely with metal clippers: ravens, deer (kind of clunky-looking), hares, and more. She nails these totems to the walls all over the place.

And then there's the quilts. She makes them, finds them, glamours people out of them, and then distributes them among the cabins. I've got five or six piled up on my bed. I like Sally's nest-building instincts. I don't have much of that myself; I'd live in a hole in the ground if I could keep it dry.

Out on the lake, a breeze was floating the island in our direction. "Danni out there?" I asked.

"Some place," Charlie said. He tries to commune with nature the way the real fairies do—they sort of merge—so he goes out to sit in the forest and then he gets deerfly bites and poison ivy. But I got to hand it to him; for a human, he really does understand. Sally said, "She'll be back for dinner because I'm making pie." Sally is a terrific cook.

We settled into silence, all staring out at the lake and the sky. I tried to quiet my mind and get myself calmed down. I usually get a peaceful feeling just from coming home, but the dirty pink sky was pissing me off. That stupid slogan from the new government campaign came into my head: "Make Your Own Happiness." As if it was that easy to just ignore the shitty outside world.

I tried to focus my mind on my home and my friends, and I tried to stop thinking about crappy things. So I watched the floating island, tracked its progress against the backdrop of trees. The aspen sisters were singing; their leaves fluttered green and silver. A light breeze ruffled the water and broke the reflection of clouds into a myriad of silver ripples. A large dark bird launched itself out of a pine and flew out over the water. Sally waved and the crow tipped its wings in response. Charlie had that intense thinking look he gets when he's about to spout a poem. He said:

"Flying bird and sky,
Island floating, golden water,
My friends, my home, I."

Sally laughed raucously, and the crow answered. Then she jumped off the porch and into the air, her long skirt whirling around her legs. She threw her arms wide and danced off over the lake, trailing her toes in the water. I watched her draw swirls of ripples in the lake's surface, breaking the reflection of the sky into patterns of black, dark green, and midnight blue.

I heard laughing out near the island. A misty shape slid out of the water and joined Sally in the dance. Their fingers touched as they spiraled around each other over the water. Then the fluttering black shape and the soft, pearly white one swirled together, round and round, and up, up, up into the sky until Sally and Danni were silhouetted against the clouds. Charlie gave a holler and threw his hat in the air.

But I didn't feel a release in my heart. The sky was still an ugly pinkish gray from the distant fires, and the air still stank of smoke. And I thought: *Someday the fire will be here.*

CHAPTER THREE:

tuesday

Just because I'm half fairy doesn't mean I don't have to make a living. I do, like everyone else. The rents on the resort are barely enough to pay the taxes, so I have other hustles like doing odd jobs with Arne.

I drove back up to Arne's trailer the next morning, parked in front, and honked. His trailer was intended for travel, but its traveling days are gone. Years ago, Arne dragged it up the dirt road and dropped it on the edge of a small, dirty turn-around for logging trucks left over from when the loggers were active. The turn-around is surrounded by straggly, skinny pines jammed together as thick as fur on a rat, none of them more than ten feet tall. It's a dead zone from a wildlife point of view; nothing can live in that mass of immature trees.

It's a good place for Arne to hide since the loggers won't be back for years, and there's no game to attract hunters. It's ugly, and I couldn't stand to live there, but I guess it suits Arne. I've never heard him complain, except to bitch about having to drive down the road to the river for water.

I like Arne, but I'm realistic about him. Arne's single because he's homely and poor. He's got an ex and some kids he never sees because they live down in Ste. Abelle, and it's too far. He isn't interested in women; they're too much trouble. He's interested in football, hockey, alcohol and marijuana, his dog, and trying to make enough money to keep the two of them fed.

So Arne lives like a hermit. I don't. I'm promiscuous; heck, I'm a wild hare. I'd rather be a coyote because they get more respect, but that's not my clan. Up here in the North Woods, we're wild hares. We fuck, we defend territory, the females raise the kids. We keep an eye out for lynxes, wolves, and hawks, and we make as many babies as we can. I don't know how many I've made. Feed, fuck, fight. That's us.

Like all the fairies, I have some special powers: enthralling, glamouring, playing with time, and flying.

Like all mixes, I'm not that good at any of the powers. I did enthrall Arne back when we were kids. He was picking on me, so I gave him a piece of gum and didn't say the words. That did it: Arne became my puppy dog, and he's been following me around ever since.

My mom was pissed when she found out. Partly she was pissed because Arne followed me home and wouldn't leave—his own folks were drunks—but mostly she was pissed because she thought enthralling was a tool to be used only as a last resort. She explained to me that Arne had not really been picking on me. He'd just been seeking attention in his clueless way, probably because he liked me. And that's probably why the enthralling worked so well; he'd wanted to latch on to someone. So now we're brothers.

Life would be a lot easier if I could just enthrall anyone who pissed me off, but I can't. I have partly enthralled people in self-defense over the years. In fact, I sometimes carry candy in my pockets for just that purpose. A piece of chocolate can make someone pretty friendly for about half an hour. It's a good way to get out of speeding tickets.

But it only works on people who are sort of inclined to get enthralled.

I use the glamour pretty often. The glamour lets me put thoughts in someone else's head, a handy skill and part of how I make a living. I gamble at the casino at Loon Lake sometimes, but not too much because I cheat by glamouring, and you can't do that too often in one place. I'm also a crackerjack shoplifter, and I don't pay my bills with local business people unless I have to. Most people aren't aware that I've conned or cheated them, but they still have a vague sense of having been played by me in some way, so I'm not popular. That's the price I pay for having spent my life in one locality.

I get by with a little cash, a little hustle, and a lot of making do. And that Tuesday morning I drove up to Arne's place because he'd found a couple of days' work and needed help.

I honked and Arne stumbled out of his trailer with a coffee cup in one hand and a cigarette in the other. And with his ridiculous poodle dancing around his feet. I got out of my car and held his coffee cup while he put the poodle back inside the trailer and said goodbye. Then we climbed into his truck and headed into town.

Lake Bear, the lake out at the big golfing resort, used to be "Bear Lake" like the town. The name got switched to sound more upscale when the mom and pop resorts started selling out and the real estate developers moved in. The fishing used to be pretty good there, but the developers took out all the marshes and didn't put in a good enough septic system so...I guess you can still fish for the planted trout if you don't mind fish that taste like dog food.

The whole damn lake is surrounded by mowed grass, docks, and concrete bulkheads. Powerboats buzz incessantly across the waters like demented lawn mowers. I have no idea why anyone would want to buy a condo there. Rumor is that people don't, that it's run for money laundering. Makes more sense.

But anyway this woman who was the resort manager wanted some landscaping done, so off we went. We pulled in at the complex headquarters, an angular building that looked like a dentist's office and had big south-facing windows, making air conditioning a necessity. We stomped right into the office in our work boots, and Arne added armpit scent to the tastefully scented air-conditioned atmosphere.

I knew before we even went in the door what kind of place it was going to be. People with money like to spend it in ways that make them feel special, exalted over mere peons like the rest of us. They like being surrounded by over-priced, over-polished, exaggeratedly classy and shiny furnishings. I was expecting mirrors and brass and got them both.

As we entered, a pretty girl in her twenties looked up from behind a desk that, sure enough, was some kind of exotic wood with metallic trim. And yes, there was a large mirror mounted on the wall behind her so patrons could watch themselves enter. The girl was local—I actually recognized her—daughter of a woman I used to date.

She saw us and smiled a tight, fake smile that clashed with the designed-to-make-you-feel-pampered furnishings. Not that the furnishings were meant to make *me* feel pampered. "Can I help you?" she asked warily. I think she recognized me but was pretending she didn't. What does a daughter say to the guy who used to be weekend fuck-buddies with her mother?

I stepped up and said, "We're supposed to meet a Mrs.

Jackson about doing some work." Arne was fading back toward the door, but I deal with intimidation by intimidating right back. Not that the girl behind the desk was the intimidation—it was the acres of polished wood, the tiled floor, and the brass pots of exotic flowers delivered from down state. And there was more intimidation from outside: the acres of mowed grass and the dead lake.

There we were, as out of place as a couple of skunks in a ballroom.

"I'll call her." The girl reached for the phone. I was tempted to leave. I get this fight-or-flight thing—I don't want to flee out of fear, but because of not wanting to break someone's nose. I was always in fights as a kid, always whacking someone over the head with a rock. Acting like a wolf, my mom used to say. She said that hares fought by being smart and devious and did not fight with violence like wolves. I can be smart and devious, but only if I think of it in time.

So I tried to think. Lots of opportunities for theft here, probably. Maybe some sabotage. I let my eyes drift out the window to the lake. The condos encircled it, making a wall of windows, patios, and flower boxes. An older couple, festooned with cameras, binoculars, and hats, strolled along the sidewalk on the lake's edge. If they were bird watchers, they were about twenty years too late.

The sky was an ugly dirty pink on account of the smoke from the afore-mentioned big forest fire about fifty miles south. I can remember when summer skies were blue. It wasn't that long ago. The only people I saw were the old couple. I wondered if maybe the complex really was a money laundering operation.

"Hello?"

I jerked, startled, and turned. A young woman stood

in the opening of the hallway to the building interior. She was completely not what I'd expected. I expected a human version of the furnishings: someone expensive, sleek, and tastefully shiny.

This gal was almost frumpy. Her hips were wide, her sweater huge and saggy, and her feet large. She gave the impression of a strong downward pull of gravity. She was wearing camping gear but not for show; the cargo slacks were not new, and the sweater was ragged along the bottom like she really went camping.

I liked her hair: not colored or permed or any of that, just lots of wavy dark brown all over her shoulders. I liked her face, too; she had a tentative smile that didn't reach her sad eyes.

"Sure, hey, hi." I stuck out my hand to shake, and she accepted it with a quick up and down and introduced herself as Taylor. Arne was still lingering by the door as if hoping for a quick exit. I waved him forward, and she shook his hand too. Then she invited us to follow her down the hall. I watched her butt as we walked. It was pretty big but alluring.

"Come in." She waved us into a small office lit by the ashy sunlight of the southern exposure. Her desk was expensively functional and obviously provided by the company, but the rest of the stuff in the office was hers. That included a jumble of well-used toys, a blankie, a large dog bed, and a sleeping child.

She smiled that sad smile and whispered, "Can you keep your voices down, please? And please have a seat?" Like everything was a question to her.

We tiptoed across the room and hunched around her desk like conspirators. She gave us papers to fill in later, which I understood to mean she didn't care if we filled them in at all. She just asked a few questions about job history and got to it: The job was to "put the garden to bed". She wanted dead stuff clipped and removed, mulch hauled in and spread, and a general neatness patrol for the flowerbeds around the office area. It was a two-day job.

The little boy curled up on the dog bed slept through our meeting. We tiptoed out again, and she gave us directions to the gardening shed.

I knew I was going to be doing most of the work since Arne's back wasn't up to much. He crawled around with a pair of clippers, clipping dead shit, while I went back and forth with the wheelbarrow, wheeling it away. Clippings went to a compost pile on the far edge of the property, and mulch came back for the flowerbeds.

We worked until Arne's watch said it was five o'clock. We'd clipped and mulched all the way around the building but not along the sidewalk leading up to the front door, so we still had work for the next day.

I heard a door snick shut with that sucking sound that goes with metal-framed glass doors, and saw Taylor Jackson hauling her kid down the sidewalk, a huge bag slung over her shoulder. They headed for an older Toyota parked at the edge of the lot. The little boy had to trot to keep up. She slung the bag into the car and slung the kid in after. Heading home to feed the kid and park him in front of the TV, most likely.

"She's been watching your butt all day," Arne commented. He cranked himself up to his feet and shook a cigarette loose from the pack.

"She was not." I was kind of embarrassed.

"That's her office window right there." He pointed with the cig. "Every time you pushed that wheelbarrow that way, she came and watched. Then she ducked out of sight when you came back." He sniggered. "Pretty funny."

"Well, how about that." I stared after the disappearing car. Possibility. I liked her.

CHAPTER FOUR:

Still tuesday

Arne and I bumped into town, his tools rattling around the back of the truck. He smoked; I didn't. The radio was on, some guy yammering about whatever. I don't listen to the news anymore since it's all owned by three or four billionaire donors to the party that always wins the elections. Then that annoying female singer came on, chirping about "Making Your Own Happiness", and I thought: *Oh no. Here we go again.*

Sure enough, as we entered town, there it was: a banner in red, white, and blue that read "YOU Can Make Your Own Happiness!!!!", and I could tell that we were going to be in for one of those god-awful national campaigns that hit the cities like a tidal wave and sent swirls of dirty flotsam and jetsam into backwaters like Bear Lake.

Arne didn't even comment on it. I didn't either. We both had our heads right up our butts when the blue lights burst alive behind us and the siren screamed. Arne stood on the brakes and yanked on the wheel. He thought we were in the way of a police chase, but I knew what was about to happen, and I didn't think I could do anything to stop it.

The police car whipped by us and screeched to a stop at an angle in front of Arne's truck. Show off. Everyone up and down the street turned to stare. Some people ducked quickly out of sight inside stores or behind cars. Arne sat stunned at the wheel.

The militiamen jumped out of the squad car, guns drawn. They wear black uniforms, black boots, and black hats—the better to look threatening. They were shouting, but I couldn't make out the words. I held my hands up and hissed at Arne, "Hands up. Stay calm."

He got his hands up, but his mouth was flapping crazily, "What? What? Oh, my God, I got some weed in my pocket. Oh, my God."

"Hush," I whispered. "Just stay calm." I could feel my own heart rate accelerating like a hot rod, but I knew that was what they wanted. They wanted to scare the shit out of us.

The militia guys flanked us, and one grabbed Arne's door and flung it open. He yelled, "Get down! Get down! Get down!"

"Go on," I tried to keep my voice low and calm. "Get on the ground. Just play along."

Arne stumbled out of the truck and fell to his knees on the road. That wasn't down far enough for the mercenary; he grabbed Arne by the hair and shoved his face into the pavement. I looked out the window to the militia guy on my side and tried to make eye contact. He was wearing shades with reflective lenses. Seems like they all do that; don't want to appear human. I stared into the black lenses and said in my glamouring voice, "Calm down. There's nothing to be excited about here. This is boring, just routine."

"Get out," he said, voice level, not shouting. I climbed out. I told him, "I can give you my ID. It's in my wallet."

"Hand it to me." He spoke like he was saying "sit" to a dog.

I have an ID. I even have a birth certificate because my

dad was human and registered my birth. And I have the new ID required to prove citizenship, which I had to buy from the fucking militia since they got the contract to run the police department and the county clerk's office. I gave him my wallet and kept talking, "This is no big deal. Just a traffic stop. Boring. Nothing exciting."

The other militia guy heard me and hollered, "Shut up!" Or maybe he was yelling at Arne. I couldn't glamour him because I couldn't see him, so I told my cop, "Tell your friend to chill out. Arne's harmless."

He handed my wallet back with a curt nod. He walked around to Arne's side, saying, "Jack, this is just a traffic stop. No big deal." I followed.

Arne was face down in the gutter. He'd twisted his head to one side and was mumbling something through the blood in his mouth. It took me a minute to figure out what he was saying: "Poochie." He wanted me to take care of his dog.

"Are you arresting him?" I asked.

"Got to," said my militia guy. "He has outstanding tickets."

"He's got marijuana too," said the other cop. He was frisking Arne. It's legal now to possess marijuana but not in a vehicle.

It's hard to glamour two people. And, while it's easy to glamour people into doing things they already want to do or things they don't care much about one way or the other, it's a lot harder to get them to do things they don't want to do. But I tried anyway, working on my militia guy first. "Hey," I said to get him to look at me. And when he glanced up or glared up—hard to tell with the shades—I said, glamouring away as hard as I could, "This is just routine. Not worth the bother. A whole lot of paperwork over nothing."

My militia guy hesitated as if the glamour was affecting

him, but then his buddy grunted, "Help me get him up." He was dragging on Arne, holding him by the handcuffs. My guy broke eye contact with me and grabbed one of Arne's arms.

So I tried to find the right words to make things easier for Arne. I said, "Forget about the weed. It's too much hassle. Just take the weed away from him. Arrest him for the ticket, that's all."

I was guessing that they'd like to have the weed for themselves. They yanked Arne to his feet and dragged him to the squad car. I called out, "Arne, I'll get your truck home and take care of your dog." I saw one militia guy shove the baggie into his pocket as he swung his fat ass into the driver's seat.

They hit the gas and roared out onto the street with a lot of unnecessary fanfare. The lookie-loos up and down the street started moving and talking. I saw a young guy who'd been hiding behind a parked car stand up and brush the dirt off his knees. His eyes met mine briefly and the corners of his mouth jerked into a sympathetic grin.

I stood there, feeling useless. Like Arne is always saying: since I'm a fairy, why can't I fix things?

CHAPTER FIVE:

tuesday Evening

Arne had left the keys in the ignition. I drove out of town slowly, fully aware that a second militia car was tracking me. They weren't being subtle about it. They hung about two car lengths back clear out to the county line. After they finally turned back, I pulled over and sat for a while, trying to get my breath back to an even rhythm. My hands were shaking. It'd been a long, long time since I'd been that angry without breaking some furniture over someone's head.

Once my hands stopped shaking, I turned around and headed back toward town. I'd deliberately driven past Arne's trailer because I hadn't wanted to lead the militia there. Not many people know he lives up there, and it's definitely best that the cops don't know. The woods are full of homeless people, but most live in the encampment along the river. There's a couple water fairy mixes that sort of guard over them and keep them from pooping and peeing too close to the water. But Arne likes to be by himself.

I drove up, parked next to my car, turned off the engine, and listened to the hysterical barking. With a sigh, I got out of the truck. Arne had a tarp up like a front porch, hanging over a fire ring. I've spent a lot of time sitting out there by a fire with friends while the rain or snow fell around us, cooking chili and drinking. Sally joins us for these drunken potlucks, along with some of the guys and gals from the camp down by the river—the water fairy guys and homeless people. And Charlie comes to Arne's parties, too, and he's the kind that talks forever once the liquor hits. Those are the good times.

But right then, in the evening with no Arne, the sight of his trailer depressed the hell out of me. I felt my energy run out onto the ground like an oil leak from a car. I slouched up to the door and hunted around until I found the key under a rock. Poochie yapped maniacally the whole time.

"Shit, dog," I snarled. Once I got the door open, Poochie attacked my leg. He's a mean little guy, even though he's mostly six pounds of hair. He bites but has no teeth. I waited while he worried my pant leg. When he finally backed off, I stepped into Arne's domain.

I have next to nothing, but I'm a fairy and we usually aren't accumulators of stuff. Sally, the raven, is an exception. Arne *is* an accumulator of stuff, but what he has is junk and dirty besides. An ancient La-Z-Boy covered with a ratty crochet throw was situated so he could spend hours staring drunkenly at a TV screen the size of a garage door. Yeah, I'm exaggerating about the size but not by much. The kitchen was buried beneath unwashed dishes, and the stink made my nose ache. The elderly couch was sagging under the weight of oily bits of machinery, rusty cardboard boxes spilling nails, and disemboweled power tools. I make it a rule to never go into his bathroom.

Poochie had been trapped inside too long and had pooped on the floor. I could smell the turds, but I couldn't see them in the murky light. "Ok, dog," I said. "We need to round up your stuff." I clambered around, stepping over boxes and heaps of junk, while keeping an eye out for lurking poop.

I gathered up a dog bed, a dog bowl, a bag of dog food, and a water bowl. That seemed like a lot of belongings for a six-pound dog. Oh, yeah, a leash. I wrapped his bed around the bowls and food, tied the bundle up with the leash, and shoved my way out the door. Poochie scrambled out and hurtled around the yard, looking for Arne. I threw all of his stuff in the back seat my car and scooped Poochie up and plopped him onto the passenger seat.

"You're gonna to stay with me awhile," I told him. He stood up on his back legs to look out the window as I drove away. Arne's truck looked desolate parked in front of his now-empty trailer. Poochie barked his distress all the way back down to the paved road, then he stopped barking and tried to crawl into my lap. Somehow that made me feel even worse.

CHAPTER SIX:

CHAPTER SIX:

tuesday Late Evening

We eat dinner together because that's our daily cycle. Fairies have lots of cycles. The dances celebrate the most important ones—the equinoxes and the solstices—but in between we do everything in cycles: the sun cycle of the day, the moon cycle of the month, the cycles of personal stuff like Sally's periods or Danni's need to get out of the water and merge with a tree, and my need to be alone at night. Charlie, even though he's human, has cycles too, though he isn't as attached as we are.

So one of our cycles is eating dinner together in celebration of another cycle: nutrients. As a hare, I'm not into eating meat. I find it nauseating. Sally eats dead flesh, though, when she's feeling feral. Hell, I've known her to cook road kill, if it was fresh. That sends both me and Charlie reeling with disgust. Charlie has been more or less copying my eating habits, even though he's Sally's thrall. He worships her, but he's always trying to be one with nature, which he interprets as being vegan.

So, with all of our individual tastes, it's complicated for Sally to put together a dinner: veggies and beans for me and Charlie, veggies and meat for her. Our routine is to all settle down in the mismatched chairs around the old wood table while Sally gives a quick ironic prayer, "Rub-a-dub-dub, thanks for the grub!" Then she cheerfully stabs her fork into a piece of dead animal.

The evening that Arne got arrested was pretty routine, except for Poochie's persistent begging. Charlie smiled at Poochie and whispered, "Sorry, nothing for you here. Ask Sally." Then he grinned across the table at her and said, "Yum, Sally. Great meal. Thanks." He's always polite like that. Never forgets.

I asked, "Where's the beer?" The cycles usually calm me down, but I was feeling pretty pissed that evening.

"Ooh, forgot!" She was ready to jump up, but I beat her to it. It's Sally's kitchen, but we all kick in to buy the stuff, so I grabbed some beers out of the fridge and plonked them down on the table. I needed to self-medicate. I slugged down a big gulp and munched into my bean burrito. Then I slugged down another big gulp.

Finally Sally said, "Okay, tell us about it." I don't drink much nowadays except at parties, so she knew something was wrong.

I wiped my mouth on my sleeve and said, "Arne's in jail for those speeding tickets he hasn't paid." The original fine was only about twenty-five dollars, and the militia had warned him that interest would build up if it wasn't paid on time. Arne had known that, after a certain amount of time, he'd go to jail if he didn't pay the fine and the interest. I'd been nagging him about it for months, and I'd even given him money once, but he spent the money on Poochie for a vet bill.

No one said anything as they thought it over. They knew that the longer Arne was in jail, the more he'd owe. Then Sally said, "We're pretty short on our kitty just now." Our kitty is what we each kick in and what we get from the tourists. We're always short.

"I'll figure it out. He's my friend." I said. I almost said he was my thrall, but I didn't know how much Charlie knew about that cake he ate, the one Sally used to enthrall him. Sally understood, though, and she nodded. "Well, keep us in mind, if the amount gets out of hand."

I was planning to keep us in mind—from the perspective that I was not going to raid our kitty unless I absolutely had to. Me and Sally and Charlie all have off-the-books hustles we do for cash. Sally sews quilts and placemats and stuff like that which she sells online or at farmer's markets, and she deals a little weed, which is legal to sell but not the way she sells it. She isn't registered and doesn't pay taxes. Besides, we don't have the setup for a real grow.

Charlie tutors online college students. Besides the odd jobs, I drive people around. We always get by somehow, but there's no slush fund for getting our friends out of jail.

Besides, Arne would think he owed it to us to pay us back, and how could he do that when he couldn't pay his fine in the first place? Maybe I could scrape up a few bucks digging under the cushions on his couch or by raiding the jar of change he kept on his kitchen counter, but real money? No. He'd never have it.

I hated thinking about money. More beer.

CHAPTER SEVEN

tuesday Night

I was walking along the shore of Lake Michigan with Taylor. The far shore, Michigan side, with the sun setting in the west. The ashy sky was a strange yellowy-gray color. The air felt heavy and moist and swirled around us in smoke-scented waves.

The beach was golden brown, a surprise to me. I liked the feel of the sand between my toes: abrasive but not bothersome, just gritty enough to make my feet tingle. Or maybe the tingle came from the water; the waves surged up the shore and left a thin trail of icy cold on the sand. I watched our footprints form and disappear as we walked along.

Ahead of us, crowds of seagulls picked bits of food out of the litter of popcorn bags and hamburger wrappers. We had our dinner packed in a traditional wicker picnic basket that I carried with the handle looped over my arm. Over my other arm I carried a blanket. We were on an old fashioned date: me, her, a meal, and a bottle of wine. Not likely to get past kissing, though.

She was wearing a long, flowing dress and a big hat, very romantic. The dress, the wind, and the waves all flapped and whirled and flowed like dancers, and I could just about pretend that the evening was all beautiful until we came to the rock.

The rock belongs on the far side of Secret Lake where I can see it from my cabin, so I was surprised to find it on the shore of Lake Michigan. But there it was, on the golden sands under the yellow-gray sky. It's huge, stands taller than me, and it's igneous: black with specks of white and gray mottled together, the embodiment in stone of a time when the whole world was on fire from volcanoes. There's a crack across the front that used to look like a lopsided smile, but now it just looks...tired. Defeated. We stood in front of the rock and held hands. I told her, "This is the rock from my lake."

I was pleased to see it. And then I noticed the tears.

The rock was crying.

I knew why, of course. I looked around at the gritty, smoky sky and the dead waters of the dying lake, and I said to Taylor, "Everything's so fucked that even the rocks are crying." I was planning to sit down there for our picnic, but she said no, it was too creepy.

Creepy. She thought a crying rock was creepy. Not sad. Creepy.

We walked away side by side, not touching, and the cold wind blew between us. Up the beach we came to a little cove where dried-out logs provided shelter. I spread the blanket out and we sat down with our backs against the logs. I watched the seagulls wheeling against the sky. Far away, a sailboat floated like a white butterfly along the line between the gray blue water and the dark blue of the distant shore. The sun was still up, but it was muted, the light dimmed by smoke into a soft reddish orange glow: a really lovely color.

Then Taylor said, "It's pretty isn't it? The sun behind the smoke."

I said, "Yes." We were quiet. I felt distant from her because of the "creepy" remark she'd made earlier about the crying rock.

Then she said, "It's very odd to be sitting here watching the end of the world while thinking of how pretty the sun looks behind the smoke, isn't it? I think humans must be unable to handle the really big things. We have to dumb things down to a size we can cope with."

She turned to me, her face earnest and scared. "We can't let ourselves really feel, can we?"

Yeah, she was right about that. I'd just seen a rock cry, but I just kept walking, looking for a place to picnic. In fact, I'd stopped thinking about the rock and had been feeling a little peeved about her "creepy" remark and about how this date was probably not going to end up with first base, let alone a home run. So yeah, I was numbing myself.

Then she said, "There's no comfort, is there?"

I thought about that. I thought about the fires, the butchered forest, the dying animals, and the dirty water, and how it was only going to get worse.

And I agreed, "No, there's no comfort."

I didn't feel distant from her anymore.

CHAPTER EIGHT:

Wednesday Morning, Early

I woke up in my cabin feeling disoriented, my mind still on the beach in Michigan. I've never been to Michigan. I have no idea why I would dream about being there with Taylor. I know why I dreamt about *her* of course; I wanted to follow up on the ass-staring. Maybe she'd like a look at the rest of me. But that didn't explain being in Michigan.

Well, the Michigan setting was probably just random sleep brain stuff, not important. But the rest of the dream—the whole sad, doomed feeling of it—seemed important. Like a message. Maybe that was about Arne?

No. Arne was part of it, but there was more. I sat on the edge of the bed and thought for a while about how I'd been in an irritable, crabby mood for what seemed like months and not just over the fires: over all the sad stuff I didn't want to think about. All the dying animals, the plants, the cycles. What Taylor said was right: The big emotions *are* too big to handle. Arne in jail just made the bad worse.

But I couldn't let some big black hole open up in front of me. I couldn't let myself fall into a funk. I had to keep on handling life because I had responsibilities: Arne, for one. So I swung my legs out of bed, planted my feet on the wooden floor, and waited until the dizziness stopped.

That woke Poochie. He sat up, gave me a look of outrage, and hopped off my bed. Then he stalked across the wood floor and flounced onto his own bed, where he should've been in the first place. With maximum drama, he tucked his nose under his tail and resumed his slumbers.

"Well, good morning to you, too," I mumbled.

Then I dragged my T-shirt off the floor, pulled it over my head, and waited on the dizziness again. This is why I rarely drink alcohol. Except at parties. Me, Sally, and Charlie had sat out on the dock drinking late, and now I was paying for it. I shoved my legs into my jeans and staggered into the bathroom.

Leaning on the sink, I had a good long stare at myself in the mirror. It's difficult for me to judge how women see me because of the glamour thing. I can make a woman think I'm drop dead sexy, or I can make them think I'm a dead fish. I don't know what they see when I'm not manipulating them.

In the mirror I saw a skinny man with lanky, dark brown hair and blue-gray eyes that were scrunched up blearily against the morning light. Weather beaten forties. Boney face, stubble, big nose. Indeterminate ethnicity. (My dad was black Irish). I have strange eyes; not so strange that regular humans run away screaming, but odd enough to put people on edge. The irises of fairy eyes are shiny, almost iridescent. We can't pass for ordinary even if we try.

I thought sardonically of Taylor and the ass-appreciation, and I wondered how appreciative she'd be after a face-to-face meet-up outside of work. Staring at an ass is one thing, but actually meeting up and dating is something else entirely. Well, I had to go out there to finish the job and get paid, so she was going to see a little more of me. I decided to shave.

After cleaning up, I took a cup of coffee out on the porch to greet the morning. I leaned on the rail, took a shot of hot liquid to the tonsils, and began to feel better. I was looking forward to fall, it's my favorite season. The leaves hadn't turned color yet, but the mornings were cool. I like the cold; the shivers make me feel alive.

The lake was calm, glassy smooth, and reflected the pinkish sky. There was a smell of smoke in the air. Maybe the fire was spreading, but sometimes lots of smoke meant the fires were dying down. Across the lake, I could see the rock on the edge of the water, blurred by the thickened air. It's part of a rocky outcrop left over from the glaciers, the southern edge of the Canadian Shield.

I swallowed the coffee faster than I usually do and took to the air. As the lake slid beneath me, I watched my reflection mingle with the reflection of the smoky sky on the water. I was a black flapping shape, distorted by ripples. I wondered if Sally felt her inner raven when in flight; hardly a day goes by that she doesn't fly. I landed with a bump and a stagger, my depth perception blunted by my hangover. My shoes scraped the moss, and I grabbed a tree branch for balance. Then I settled down on my haunches, poised on the tip of the rock, and contemplated the lake.

I've always loved the rock. Even when I was a little kid, I'd fly out to the rock to think or to get away from my dad. Most of the time he was pretty mellow, but sometimes he'd get really angry from the thoughts in his head: conspiracy theories. He thought "Reds" were taking over Washington DC. This was back in the nineteen-eighties, so he was right, but decades too soon. Mom could control him, mellow him out, but she'd let him rant on sometimes just to let him be himself, I guess.

I don't really know what she saw in him—besides a human to own the land on her behalf—unless it was the music and the stories. My dad was a great singer, storyteller, and guitar player. He had an act he did at the casino and at the Elks and places like that: sang ballads, told some of the history behind the ballads, that sort of thing. Folk music. Storytelling is a big thing with fairies, so that was something he had in common with my mom and the hare clan.

But he was a mean drunk, and he drank whenever he could. He ruined his act by getting drunk on stage and ranting at the audience. He ranted at home, too, with the radio on some hate talk show all about how bums were wasting tax dollars, and immigrants were raping nice white girls, or conspiracy theories. I think he really believed that stuff. And he added in his own dark fantasies. My mother would put up with it for a while, then she'd shut him down by making him sleepy.

When I was a kid, I wasn't sure if I was going to grow up to be a mean drunk like my dad or a hare like my mom. She made me go to school and learn human stuff, but she took me to the dances regular. I mean the fairy dances. Every equinox and solstice we'd be out in the woods on one of the remote lakes up by the border, dancing. We'd go into fairy time, so we could raise a ruckus and not be noticed.

The real fairies like my mom and Danni don't have an existence like I have. They come from the cycles of life and death, kind of like music comes from the vibration of vocal cords or poetry comes from the firing of neurons in Charlie's head. They don't exist on their own. They'd say that none of us do, including humans. They say that we all are just temporary manifestations of the cycles. But when the cycles are broken, they're the first to go.

The dances are celebrations of the cycles, the grand rhythms of the seasons and the movements of stars and planets, the cycles of life and death: the nutrient cycles, the prey/predator cycles, all of the growth through the stages of life to death and decay. It's all very religious but not solemn. Heck, no, not solemn at all. In fact, it's hard to tell a fairy dance from a drunken blow-out. Everyone gossips and tells stories. Sometimes the guys fight while the gals gather in groups with the kids or go off with some of the guys. Yeah, there is an orgy aspect to it. Especially with the hares, all the fighting and fucking. But the coyotes can get rambunctious too.

I like spending time with the hare clan, the pure forest fairies. When our kind of fairies manifest as visible, they look sort of human but sort of hare-like. It's hard to point at one aspect and say, "That's the hare in them." They don't have big ears, for example. But they do give the impression of muscle and bone and fur, wariness and sneakiness, impulse and action. My mom, when she was visible, was sexy as hell in a gypsyish way.

All of the fairies used to talk with the Native Americans, tell stories, even dance with them—at least that's what the older fairies say. I mean back in the day, long ago. But starting with the pioneers or maybe before that, they started thinking that they'd better be secret from humans, so that's the tradition now: stay secret. My mom drilled that in me every single school day—don't use any powers at school, don't tell anyone about us, and don't mingle too much with humans.

Study people, use them, but don't get close. People are wolves, she said. That from a fairy who married a human!

But she was right; it is important to study people. They are stronger, dominant. If they knew about our powers, they'd either kill us off or try to use us for their own benefit. The truth is our powers are nothing compared to the power of human greed and stupidity. And money, the most powerful magic of all.

Humans have the power to kill everything. Humans are

killing everything.

That's when I felt the water under my hand.

I lifted my fingers in surprise; my hand was wet, smeared with water and pine needles. Then I looked down at the rock. The top was fuzzy with dark green moss and crusted with orange and yellow lichens, now damp and leaking a thin stream of water that slid down over the steep jagged rock's face in fingers like raindrops running down the window.

The rock was crying.

I couldn't comprehend it. At first I just couldn't make the rock's tears real in my mind. I stroked the rock, got my fingers wet, licked the cold, clear water. I kept feeling along the edge of the moss, searching for the beginnings of the rock's tears until my knees and socks were wet too. Then I pushed myself up to my feet and looked out over the lake.

The aspen sisters were singing on the far side, their leaves glittering silver and green. A gentle breeze slipped through the trees, answering their song with gentle laughter. Under the water, trout patrolled for bugs. Danni was down there somewhere.

I thought about all of the years I'd lived by the lake, all of the time I'd spent on my rock, all of the music I'd heard from the aspens and the breezes. Then I thought about the forest fires, the butchered landscape, and the dying lakes up north polluted by the mining. I thought about the hot summers and the too-warm winters. And I remembered Taylor's words in the dream: "There is no comfort."

Something hardened up inside of me into a sharp stony point, like one of those rock spearheads the Native Americans used to make. I could feel the spear point in the back of my throat, and it hurt. I could feel spears in my arms and legs and sharp points behind my eyes. I stood up straight and rigid, not my usual way of standing, and I made a vow: I was going to get Arne out of jail, but more than that, I was going to war. With all of them. With all of the humans. I was going to pay Arne's way out of jail, and then I was going to make the fuckers pay *me*.

CHAPTER NINE:

Wednesday Morning, Later

I flew back to Sally's cabin but kept within the trees in case the tourists were up. Turns out I was right; they were on her porch checking out, so I walked up to the cabin. I could hear the guy's voice because he was loud. He was asking Sally if they had a tight line over the lake. She said no, and he asked how she could hover over the water. She just said she didn't do any hovering and gave him the bill. I joined them on the porch.

Sally is pretty in an unkempt way: lots of curly hair, wears skirts and peasant blouses. The tourist was giving a bit too much attention to her chest which was pissing the wife off. Sally held out her hand for the payment, and he gave her the charge card. She disappeared into the cabin to run the card, and the wife gave the guy a look that would've burned a hole in him if he hadn't been too hung over to notice.

"Did you two have a nice stay?" I was feeling snarky, so I used a fakey friendly tone. The wife scowled, but the guy said with lumbering insouciance, "Yeah sure. It's really relaxing out here." He put some lust, or the pretense of lust, into that "relaxing" and licked his lips. I decided to fuck with him.

Sally emerged with the receipt, all business, but he gave

her a too-big smile, and his hand closed on hers. She let go of the receipt, yanked her hand back, and said through her teeth, "You guys come back soon, OK?" with sparks shooting out of her eyes. Then she turned her back on him and retreated. He smirked and rolled his tongue around his lips. "It sure must be nice to live out here." Rolled his eyes in Sally's direction.

I said, "Yeah, but you need to pay the whole bill."

"What? I paid." He stepped back, startled.

"You haven't paid me back for the beer I bought for you or the groceries." I kept my tone light but firm, matter-of-fact, but I was glamouring hard.

"I bought that beer!" He was getting purple-faced. "I got it in that little Podunk town up the road."

"And you drank it all, and then you bought some more from us. Shit, don't stiff us for eleven lousy bucks." I sneered at him, which was easy because I honestly thought he was a cockroach. He stared with his mouth open. The wife didn't say anything, just looked disgusted. I'll bet she went to bed and left him up drinking, so she believed my story. She was sneering at him too.

"Hey," he backed down, shrugging like it was no big deal. "I forgot, okay? Sheesh, don't make a federal crime out of it."

He dug out his wallet and gave me a twenty. I glamoured at him to make him tell me to keep the change, and he did. I shoved the money in my pocket. The man frowned, sure he'd been screwed but not sure how. I watched the emotions struggle on his face and saw him decide on a pose of indifference. He nodded in Sally's direction, and joked, "Well, keep on enjoying the scenery. I liked it up here a lot."

"Well, I don't like it," snapped the wife. "No TV

reception."

"Who needs TV?" The guy was answering his wife but didn't look at her. Sally yelled from inside the cabin, "Phone's ringing!" We have what must be the last landline in the U.S. I said, smiling meanly, "Have a safe drive home," and escaped.

Hey, I know twenty bucks isn't much, but I never claimed to be anything more than small time. And it was twenty bucks toward getting Arne out.

CHAPTER TEN:

Still Wednesday

I drove up to Bear Lake, careful to stay below the speed limit, using my car to save on Arne's gas. Besides, his truck was always on the brink of breakdown, and it was going to be hard enough to get him out of jail without having to raise money for repairs too.

But the most important reason why I drove the car was a bit of luck: just when I needed some money, Mrs. Allen called. Well, it was the first of the month and she always called, but I'd forgotten because of all the stress over Arne. So her call came as a fortunate surprise when I needed one.

She always wanted the same thing: a ride into town to the little mom and pop North Woods Motel. And a ride home the next day. She was one of my regulars because I took her to church every Sunday too. And home again.

We often discussed comparative theology. She's a Christian, but in her own weird way that didn't really match the church she went to. She went to one of those real true we-are-right-and-everyone-else-is-wrong Bible churches located in a white clapboard building that used to be a grange hall.

As a pagan, I'm not really the one to evaluate how Christian someone is. I just knew there was some tension between her and the pastor because she always got this school teachery look on her face when I asked about his sermons. Like she was about to give someone a D on their essay for doing a half-assed job. She used to teach history at the high school where I was a lousy student.

I asked once her why she went to that church, and she said she had friends there and liked the music. I always wondered if her friends knew about her monthly motel visits. I mean, what was up with that? Her husband was dead, so she was fancy-free, but sheesh, she was eighty if she was a day.

Mrs. Allen lived about five miles outside Bear Lake in a trailer park that's really gone downhill. I can remember when it was a retirement village, lots of old folks outside in the summer in their lawn chairs, grandchildren running wild all over. A happy place, with lots of flower gardens and people sort of putzing around, visiting each other.

Now it's overrun with homeless cats, and every driveway is occupied by a dead or dying car. Narrow-eyed suspicious children stopped their play and stared as I drove by, keeping an eye out for the militia. The trailer park is subject to periodic raids. Mrs. Allen was one of the few old folks still hanging on to respectability there.

I pulled into her driveway and observed the flower baskets hanging from her porch: nearly bloomed out but still pretty. Her lawn was mowed and her porch was a picture in white whicker furniture and fake pink roses in bowls. I didn't have to honk or get out of the car; she bustled out with her purse over her arm. She looks like everyone's grandma, but I think she plays that up. It's her way of glamouring people. Mrs. Allen is one of the very few humans I actually like.

I got out and opened the car door for her, and she smiled that secretive smile, playing little old lady to my gentleman. We'd been playing that game for months. Once in, I asked, "Heading down to the motel, Mrs. Allen?" I was hinting that I'd like to know why she had that routine. She answered casually, "Why yes, just my usual trip." As if that was a real answer.

I drove slowly past the suspicious children and out to the road while trying to think of another way to fish for an explanation. "The owners, they friends of yours?"

"Oh, I am a regular, so I know them, but not really friends."

I could glamour her but that would ruin the fun of our routine. I was curious as hell. Did she meet a lover? I couldn't quite picture that, but why else spend a night in a motel once a month?

"I'm surprised the place is still open." I commented.

"Angie and Martin will be retiring soon. They're going to move south when they close up." See how she was willing to gossip about Angie and Martin while not saying anything about herself? Mrs. Allen was a master at deflection.

"Are you going to the parade Saturday?" she asked.

"What parade?" I got right up to fifty-five but not a fraction over.

"The 'Make Your Own Happiness' parade, of course." She laughed and I got the impression that there was some irony there, like she was laughing *at* the parade. But I could've been imagining it.

"No, probably not. I hope I'll have some work that day."

"Oh, that's disappointing. The militia will be on parade." Again with the touch of irony. I glanced at her, but she was looking out her window. I wondered if her comment was a warning. The militia definitely notes who attends these government events and who doesn't. Or maybe she really was just disappointed on my behalf.

"Sorry, no," I said. Then I fished a bit to see what she would say, "I don't like crowds anyway."

"I suppose the whole town will turn out. I hear Congressman Van Dusen is going to make an appearance," she commented. Her tone was neutral.

"Really? I didn't think there were enough votes out here to attract him." I was really fishing now.

And I got a bite. "He has friends staying at the resort," she told me. "They're Russians. Trade commissioners." Yeah, there was irony in her tone all right. She said "trade commissioners" as if she was saying "dogshit purveyors."

I matched her trade commissioners up with the money laundering rumor and got a politician and his donor friends visiting the development that laundered the donations from Russia. We're out in the sticks here, but even the smaller party fish are in with the Russians; just smaller Russian fish, I assume. The really big deals go on in DC.

I wondered if I could get her to say something a little more open about how she sees things but the "Report Illegal Aliens" billboard hove into view. We stared in silence at the swarthy man and his mysterious wife, then rolled on into town.

I pulled into the North Woods Motel and tried once again to see the attraction. It'd never been much in the first place and had gone down hill in recent years: just a single story row of lookalike rooms facing a parking lot. Some asters were blooming in a planter outside the office in an attempt to dress the place up. There were two cars parked in front of rooms—a busy day for the motel. Mrs. Allen always got the same room, the one in the middle. That was one small fact that I'd managed to weasel out of her.

She paid me—over-paid, actually, she always does—and tipped me and gave me her Cheshire Cat smile. I watched her walk up to the office door. She was still pretty mobile for her age and walked with her back straight, but, even with those signs of good health, I couldn't believe she was having a monthly tryst with a boyfriend.

Oh well, not my business, I thought.

My business was to make some money. I had to figure out how to get Arne out of jail and how much that was going to cost. The fine was probably about fifty bucks because of the interest, but he was also being charged room and board so the total bill was going up every day. So I was in kind of a race—I had to get the money to spring him and the longer it took to raise the money, the more I'd have to raise.

And I couldn't just glamour him out of jail because sooner or later someone would notice that he hadn't actually paid. There'd be a problem with the county accounts, and he'd just get arrested again. I was assuming that the militia kept records of things like fine payments since they do stuff that used to be run by the city government. They're a bunch of assholes, but I didn't think I could count on them being completely incompetent at record-keeping.

The militia is basically a gang. Everyone would see them as a gang for sure if they weren't white, but they are, so their gang behavior is accepted as good and American. They're a bunch of wannabe macho jerks who used to all wear black jackets decorated with American flags back when they were just bikers.

They called themselves the Sons of Odin and did unofficial law enforcement—really harassing anyone they thought was an immigrant—before they got the contract to be the police department. The old police were mostly members of the gang before privatization, so really it was a change that wasn't a change.

They also run a gun shop and shooting range. All of that—

the county contract, the so-called policing, the shop and range—makes them the most economically secure people in the community. They're parasites, actually.

So I couldn't glamour the whole gang and I couldn't fight the whole gang, which meant I had to pay them. And that meant getting more cash than I usually had and that meant finishing up the job at the condos.

And that's why I was in a really, really pissy mood as I made my way to Lake Bear.

CHAPTER ELEVEN:

Wednesday Afternoon

As I drove, I watched my gas gauge sinking, and my pissy mood got worse. It never fails: As soon as I have an urgent need for money, I also get an urgent need to spend it on stuff I don't want to spend it on. I hate living like that, always staggering from one nickel and dime crisis to the next. That burning feeling in my stomach got worse. I wanted a cigarette, not because I smoke, but because I wanted to burn something up and stub something out.

So it was in a cloud of black thoughts that I parked my shitty, dirty old car right smack in front of the glossy front doors of fucking Lake Bear Resort and Golf Course and ejected myself from the front seat, slamming the door for good measure. There were several men inside. I could see them through the glass: large men wearing the kind of clothes city people purchase for wearing in the country so they can experience the wilderness in the right outfit. Not that there was any actual fucking wilderness left, the assholes.

So I pushed the door open and stalked in, ready to throw back at them whatever attitude they threw at me. To my surprise, their attitude was friendly. The gal at the desk said happily, "Oh, here he is now! It's Mr. Fallon." And the leader of the guy group turned toward me and held out his hand to shake.

Okay, so they were friendly. Still assholes. The friendliness just meant they wanted something. I scanned them and realized that Leader of the Assholes was my Congressman, Mr. Tom Van Dusen, and the flanking members of Team Asshole had to be those out-of-town money launderers Mrs. Allen told me about. They were all well-fed, big, white guys with neatly cut hair and well-tended teeth. Teeth are a class marker: Arne doesn't have any, and most people around here have some but need dental work. Only those hooked into the money stream have big, shiny, white smiles.

I took the bastard's hand and shook it. Then I stepped back and waited.

"Glad to meet you. Mr. Fallon, is it? I'm Tom Van Dusen, and these are my friends Mike and Alex."

I didn't need to hear them speak to know they were Mikhail and Alexei. We did more handshaking as Tom went on to explain their business. "Tammy says you're local, born and raised here, and might know where to do some hunting. Mike and Alex are looking for bear." He laughed, "They're loaded for bear!" Joke. The two Russians didn't get it, but they responded with heh heh heh anyway. "So could you set us up with a guide or perhaps guide us yourself? For a consideration, of course."

A thought burst into my head, a beautiful vision. I saw a pile of money. Potentially a big pile of money. But I didn't want to seem too eager, so I said, "It's not bear season, not yet."

Tom grinned, "I'm sure we can work something out about that? Mike and Alex are only going to be here for a week, and I was hoping to show them the best of the North Woods. It's all about hunting and fishing up here, isn't it?"

Actually, except for deer, the hunting sucks. The fleas

and ticks killed off the moose, and the hunters killed off the bears, and the loggers fucked the forest up for everything else. Idiots think that if they see a lot of trees, it means they're looking at nature.

I said, "I can't get you a bear because it's not the season, but I know some good fishing places. Pike. I can get you some northern pike." And I indicated with my head that we should move down the hallway. "I'm on my way to see Taylor."

He picked up on my tactics right away. Probably spent half his life in hallways making illegal deals. "Sure, fishing, that's a good idea. Pike, you boys will love that!" he said, making herding motions at the Russians. We all started edging toward the hallway, talking about fish.

I had no intention of taking anyone bear hunting. I just wanted some flexibility in case I could figure a way to get more money out of them than just by being a fishing guide. So as soon as we were out of earshot of Tammy, I asked, "How much are we talking here? Because I could get jail time for poaching. And the militia loves having people inside."

He laughed, "Business is good for the militia? You ever been a customer?"

"No," I said, staring him straight in the face.

The smile dropped off his face, "Okay. How about five hundred for the fishing and an extra thousand for the extra trouble?" By which he meant the bear hunting out of season. I tried to look hesitant, but not *too* hesitant, so I just said, "Look, I'm taking you fishing, but we'll go where we might see a bear. Go ahead and talk about the fishing but keep the bear part private. Okay? You're a Congressman," I told him, "but I live up here."

I could tell they liked the secrecy aspect. Then he said,

"How about half now and half on our trip? And a bonus if we get a bear?" He pulled out his wallet and started peeling off bills. Show off. No, that's wrong; he'd done this so many times that he *wasn't* showing off. Paying cash for shady transactions came naturally to him. This deal was tiny potatoes.

I took the two-fifty and reminded him, "Remember this is a fishing trip. The bear is a maybe." He replied that what with their obligations to the upcoming parade and meetings with local officials they were busy, but after that they were on vacation. I said, "Okay, how about Sunday? And don't tell anyone."

So it was settled. We worked out the details of when and where to meet, and I got my good buddy Tom the Congressman's cell phone number and shook hands again with everyone, and then I got the hell away from them. They headed back to the lobby in a little herd.

I moved down the corridor a couple of steps, then stopped and leaned against the wall. I told myself: *You did good. Wild hare, not wolf. Mom would approve.* I went over it again in my head: I'd get them out to the lake on Sunday. They'd pay me the rest of the five hundred, and then I'd figure some way to scam the thousand out of them too. Get them drunk. Then get them to hand over a couple hundred more or win it at poker. With Sally's help, I'd bullshit it out of them some way.

But that was just the fishing on Sunday part of the plan. The bear hunting—I wasn't really worried about getting busted for poaching. For one thing, we weren't ever really going to hunt a bear. But I wanted options. I wanted the possibility of getting them out on a bear hunt that no one knew about, so I could do something to them that would not be connected to me. Nothing definite in mind...maybe just another option for getting another thousand. Like get them lost and make them pay me to rescue them?

Possibilities.

I'd been in a really shitty mood, but life had just handed me a big bouquet of opportunities for cash and revenge. Mrs. Allen's God moving in mysterious ways? Nah. I don't believe in that kind of god. I told Mrs. Allen once that it didn't matter if her God existed or not since He was so damn ineffective. She said that God was not responsible for our lousy choices. And I said that apparently He's not responsible for saving our asses either, so it doesn't matter if He exists or not. We enjoy this kind of banter.

Bottom line: I was going to get another two-fifty on Sunday, stood a good chance of getting more, and had the possibility of using an imaginary bear hunt to get even more than that. So thank you to whoever brings good luck to bad people like me.

I unclenched my fists and went looking for Taylor.

She was in her office, but this time the kid was awake. He was mindlessly banging a plastic dinosaur against the side of the desk, apparently because he liked the sharp crack of hard plastic against wood. Or maybe he liked the spider web of cracks he was making in the varnish. Taylor glanced up from her paperwork as I entered, her face lined with exhaustion. I wondered if the kid had kept her up all night banging on things. He was really into repetitive, annoying noises.

She said, "Oh, hi, Mr. Fallon. Come in." She didn't tell the kid to be quiet. I could tell she'd given up on that battle. So I sat down, pulled up a chair, and once again I was leaning over her desk like a conspirator, but this time it was so we could hear each other without shouting.

"Arne's in jail," I told her. Her expression said: Arne

who? "My partner, from working yesterday. He's in jail for a traffic ticket."

"Oh, I'm sorry to hear that." She looked genuinely concerned. "Will he be able to get out soon?"

"Yeah, probably, if I can raise the money. I'm going to finish the job today, but can you pay me right away?"

"Sure. Come by when you're done."

"Can you give me Arne's too? So I can use it to spring him?" I started glamouring her.

She looked hesitant. She was thinking that Arne and I were friends or seemed to be friends...So I pushed the glamour harder, "We're friends. It's OK. I will use the money to get him out of jail. And we need cash."

Her face cleared, "Okay. I was going to offer cash anyway."

I was halfway out to the shed before I realized that my shitty mood had come creeping back. And after a pause for thought, I realized why: because I had glamoured her. I didn't mind fucking with the Congressman, but Taylor seemed so tired and sad that I felt bad about fucking with her.

I've had lots of girlfriends. My pattern was to meet someone and have fun for a while: good sex, good food, no fights. But I never stuck around. A couple months with one gal was enough. So I was in between girlfriends then and, yeah, I was thinking about Taylor as a possibility. The bad dream had left me feeling close to her, closer than we really were—which was not close at all. I barely knew the woman.

I just knew I liked her, so I felt bad about glamouring her into doing something she'd probably fret about. She'd probably start worrying about the money, wondering why she agreed to something so stupid as to give one person's earnings in cash to another person. I thought of her hunched over her desk with that annoying banging going on while she tried to keep her mind off her worries and get some work done.

I had worries, too, and worrying about her was distracting me from worrying about Arne and my hare-brained plan. As I hacked the clippers at dried flower stalks, I tried to focus my thoughts. I had two-fifty plus my pay and Arne's pay and the taxi money. Minus the gas money, that came to... about four-twenty, give or take. So I could get Arne out of jail right away. Then I'd get more out of those assholes just because I wanted to fuck them over.

I burned my way through the entire flowerbed from the parking lot to the front door while trying to figure out how to turn the secret bear hunt into a robbery. Then I got up, my knees creaking, and headed for the wheelbarrow and the mulch. As I passed her window, I took a quick peek and my eyes met Taylor's. She ducked her head in embarrassment, then realized that ducking her head was itself an embarrassing behavior, so she lifted her chin and gave a defiant wave. I thought: *You poor mouse. Some hawk is going to eat you. But not me. I'm not a hawk.*

After that, I pushed the wheelbarrow back and forth without looking at the window. I got the whole fucking flowerbed all covered with thick, dark compost, ready for the winter. Usually, I feel pretty good after gardening, but that day I just felt anxious to get moving. I wiped my hands on my jeans and went inside.

Thank goodness, the kid had fallen asleep. Taylor hissed "shhh" at me the minute I stepped in the door. I've noticed that some kids seem to have an on or off switch and nothing in between. I tiptoed elaborately to the chair, hunched over and really hamming it up to make her laugh, and she did giggle a bit. I sat down even though I didn't need to since really all she had to do was hand me the money. But I thought I'd give conversation a chance to start.

I whispered, "How long's he been asleep?"

"Just a few minutes."

I wanted to ask her how she could live with the noise. Or couldn't she sedate him? But those aren't good things to ask to a mother. Instead I said, "He seems very active and healthy."

To my surprise, she snorted derisively. "Yeah, that's the tactful way to put it." We shared a grin.

"Do you have any kids?" she asked. I couldn't tell her that I did, but I didn't keep track of how many, so I said, "Nope. Not married either."

"Neither am I." She grimaced. "Divorced."

Then she shifted back in her chair, uncomfortable, I think, at how off task from business the conversation had gone. "You'll be wanting your money. Hey, I'm sorry, and I understand the problem, but I really can't give out your friend's money in cash. Since he needs his money now, I wrote a check out to him." She had my cash and Arne's check ready in two labeled envelopes. She pushed the envelopes across the table.

I thought: *Shoot*. Could be a hassle, depending on how much I needed for Arne, since I didn't want to take the time to get him to endorse it and then go to a bank. So I deducted his sixty-six dollars and got...three-sixty. That should be plenty. She was smiling apologetically.

"No problem." I grinned at her as I scraped up the two envelopes. Then, on impulse, just to extend the conversation, I asked, "Hey, there's a rumor that this place is a money laundering operation. Any truth to that?"

She almost panicked. Her mouth dropped open, her eyes cut toward the wall, and she gibbered. "No, No! I never heard anything like that!"

"Okay then," I backed off the topic quickly. I got to my feet, surprised by how tired I felt. "None of my business anyway. Thanks for giving us the work." I was nodding and smiling at her, trying to get her to smile back.

"Well, thank you." She didn't smile. "I'll call if more work comes up?" She said that like it was a question.

"Sure," I agreed. "That would be great. See you later." And I quietly stepped over and around toys on my way out the door.

CHAPTER TWELVE:

Wednesday, Early Evening

I went to the county annex building to see Arne. The jail is a low gray building from the 1950s, with measly narrow windows and barberry bushes trimmed to rigidity flanking the front door. There's the inevitable flagpole with an American flag flying above the militia flag. I considered that for a few minutes. The police flag and the nation's flag. I also considered the name above the militia building door: "County Building One." Then I looked across the street. Yeah, the county courthouse was two and the municipal building where the City Council meets was three. Interesting pecking order.

I gathered myself, got my temper under control, and strode up to the door. The only way to deal with bullies is to stand up to them, so I marched in full of attitude and ran right up against the little old lady that used to be the county clerk. She was hunched at her computer, blinking at the screen, frowning while her fingers jumped compulsively over the keyboard. Startled by my entry, she jerked back in her seat and looked up.

"Oh hi, there." She shoved her glasses up her nose. "Can I help you?"

Okay, so I had to back off. I had expected to be dealing with a militiaman, not a little old lady. I leaned against the counter. "I've come to pay the fees for Arne Svenson."

"Arne Svenson?"

"Yes."

"I'm real sorry," she said, "but there's no staff here right now. Can you come back tomorrow?" She blinked apologetically.

"What? No staff?" I was flummoxed. "I can't get him out today?"

"No, I'm sorry, not after five. See the time? You need to come in between nine and five." She was still smiling hard at me, as if pleading for my patience.

I tried to stay reasonable. "But you're open right now."

"I'm here until six," she explained. "And so are some of the law enforcement officers, but the jail is closed."

I let that sink in and tried not to go ballistic. With elaborate courtesy, I asked, "Can you tell me how much he owes to get out?"

"Oh no, that's confidential. He'd have to tell you." She shook her head, wide-eyed at the prospect of violating a prisoner's privacy. I was beginning to think the so-apologetic demeanor was an act. I let my face harden.

"So how much is the fee for each day?" I glamoured her into giving me a straight answer because I was tired of fooling around.

"That's one twenty-five," she said.

"One twenty-five!" My patience snapped and I just plain yelled at her. "What was this place, the frickin' Waldorf-Astoria?" Blinking frantically, she leaned away from me. I realized that my body language was communicating rage, so I tried to rein myself in a bit by speaking slowly and carefully, "So I know his fine is about fifty bucks, so that would be about one hundred seventy-five today, but three hundred tomorrow. More or less, right?"

"I don't . . . I can't say. You'll have to ask Mr. Svenson."
Blink. Blink. Blink.

I had a sudden thought, "Wait . . . he got arrested on
Monday. So does he have to pay for Monday too?"

"The day starts at nine o'clock," she said. "That's when
breakfast is served, so each day runs from nine to nine. But
if the prisoner leaves before nine a.m., that day doesn't
count."

Jesus H. Christ. They had their schedule set up for
maximum extortion. So Arne had Monday, even though he
got busted after five in the evening, plus Tuesday, plus
today, so I'd have to be there before nine Thursday with
four hundred and twenty-five dollars.

I could do it, but it would take every penny I had plus
Arne's check. Which was a problem because I couldn't cash
Arne's check before nine, so we'd get charged for Thursday,
and I was not going to have enough money with Thursday
added on.

She saw the look on my face and rushed an explanation.
"The guilty people have to pay to run the jail. I mean why
shouldn't they? Why should the taxpayers have to do it? And
it isn't just room and board. It's salaries and equipment
and, well, everything the community needs." Her chin was
up. A look of righteousness stiffened her soft, doughy face.
"So I am very sorry if Mr. Svenson has to pay for his time
here, but he shouldn't have—"

The stupid woman didn't know how close I was to kicking
her face in. I let my hands open and spread my fingers out
in the opposite of a fist. I leaned over the counter until
my face was in her personal space, and I said, enunciating
carefully, "Thank you for your help." And then, glamouring
as hard as I could, I thought at her: *You just peed on*

yourself. All over.

I saw her body contract and her thighs clamp together. Her eyes rolled around frantically.

And you think you have cancer. In fact you KNOW you have cancer. Of the cervix.

Bitch.

I drove home in a state of anger that I managed to keep just short of road rage. I made the turn onto our road but found no comfort in the green cathedral of our old forest. I tried. I slowed the car down to a crawl, rolled the window down, and hung my left arm out to feel the air. I inhaled the scents. I squinted at the sky and noticed that the pinkish shade was gone. The sky was actually blue, a bright robin's egg color, full of early evening light.

The fire must've burned out, or maybe the wind had shifted. It was good to see blue after so many weeks of ashes and smoke, but I had to tell myself it was a good thing, practically order myself to feel appreciation. What I really felt was: *So fucking what if the sky is blue, everything else sucks.*

I mentally totaled the fees up again: five hundred dollars anytime before five on Thursday. I wouldn't get the rest of the fishing trip payment until Sunday. By Monday, Arne's fee would be up to eight-seventy five, if I was doing the math right. So I had to get that thousand, not for revenge, but for just paying off the militia for Arne.

No comfort. Isn't that what Taylor said in the dream?

The car lurched around the last corner, and the lake came into view: ripples of gold glitter on deep blue water.

65

I parked and walked around to the front of my cabin and sat down.

From my porch, I stared out at the lake and I smelled it and felt the dampness in the air. The needles from the pines blow off and fall into the water. Leaves, needles, and little branches make a sodden matrix on the lake floor. Tiny life forms procreate, eat, and are eaten by little fish. And everything eats the little fish: bigger fish, herons, loons, kingfishers, weasels, river otters, bald eagles . . . and those creatures die at some point and are reincarnated as fodder for bugs and topsoil. And residual nutrients get rained into the soil and get sucked up by the trees. That's the simple version of a cycle; it's all much, much more complex than that.

My mother knew all about the cycles. She taught me about how us fairies are nature spirits and how we only exist where nature exists. My mother died when the timber company cut down the forest across our property line. She needed more forest than I do.

There are no fairies out at Lake Bear.

The problem was not just Arne being in jail, or the town being sold to the militia, or the constant fires all summer. It was bigger, deeper, and wider than that. The cycles were broken. I'd known this truth for many years—after all, I'd been watching the break down all my life—but somehow the reality really slammed me at that moment. What had Taylor said? That we cannot handle the big issues and problems? We have to dumb everything down to a level we can stand? I could not, at that moment, protect myself. I let it in, let all the tragedies steamroller over me like a great monstrous machine, stomping on my heart.

And then I remembered how Danni took care of people who pissed her off.

CHAPTER THIRTEEN:

thursday Before Dawn

The wind had shifted and the air was prickly with ash. The moon was a soft diffuse gold though the hazy starless darkness. Danni and I flew through the smoke-scented sky of early morning, maybe four a.m. The forest was an undifferentiated mass of black below us. Far away to the north winked a few lights: Bear Lake. We were flying between the blue-black of the sky and the dense wooly black of the forest.

It was chilly. The air slid under my collar, across my chest, and down my sleeves. I was flying and shivering at the same time. Damn it, I should've thought about how cold it would be up in the sky in the dark. We were in search of a place just outside our property line where an old logging road wandered back into the second growth timber.

Danni flitted over to me and touched my hand. She was nearly invisible, appearing only as glistening blue lines in the light of the moon. She tapped my hand and then her face. I heard her in my head saying: *This is the place.* Good thing she'd spotted it, because I never would've. Not from the sky. We grabbed hands and shifted into fairy time.

I don't know how to explain fairy time to someone who can't do it. It's almost like a change in attitude, a mind thing, but it's real. I felt a little lurch of dizziness, and then we were in a different place, a space Danni made years ago when I helped her get rid of some trappers.

We circled low and flew just above the tree tops. I scanned the dark forest, looking for a change in the darkness that would indicate a clearing.

A light pierced the night and blinked away. I grabbed for Danni and pointed, but she'd already seen it. The light reappeared a bit off to one side. We slid down between the trees to just above the underbrush, and, using the light as a guiding beacon, we wended our way between trees until we were on the edge of a clearing.

They had a campfire lit just as they'd had years ago. Two men were hunkered down in low-slung camp chairs. The smell of coffee and cigarettes wafted in the air along with the stink of dried blood—well, I might've imagined that part. I could hear their voices, low mumbles. One reached out for the coffee can and poured himself a drink.

They looked reasonably content, at least from a distance. I wasn't sure how I felt about that. I didn't want them to suffer continuously, but I didn't want them to live happily ever after either. Actually, I was surprised to find them alive at all. I'm not sure how fairy time works, except it's a lot slower than regular time. I called out, keeping my voice calm and chummy, "Hey there, you mind getting a visitor? Can I join you?"

They both scrambled to their feet, arms out as if they were going to grab for their guns. But their guns were gone, had been for years.

"Who's there?" one yelled.

"Just me. I'm friendly," I said. Danni had vanished, but I knew she was still beside me. A murky dawn gray was creeping into the sky overhead, but it was still dark in the forest. I landed on the ground and waded through the ferns with one arm up in a wave. The two guys watched me warily.

I'd never really looked at them, not as individual people. To me and Danni, they'd just been trappers. Now I looked, and I saw that they were probably relatives, father and son maybe. The older version was grizzled, fat, and friendly while the younger one was more hostile, only about twenty-five, and had a permanent look of grievance.

"Hey," the younger one called, with a belligerent tilt of his chin. "Who are you?"

"Are you lost?" the father asked. "We're kind of lost."

"Bob Fallon," I said. "I live around here. No, I'm not lost."

When last I saw these two guys, Danni had brained one with a rock, and I had slammed the other on the side of his head with his gun. They'd been setting traps in the National Forest and had crossed onto our land. We'd located them by flying, and then we attacked them and left them unconscious. We stashed them in fairy time so they could never trap on our land again.

And there they were, getting their morning coffee.

"What happened?" I asked. "Looks like you got hit by something."

"Oh, yeah." They both felt their wounds with their fingers. Dried blood was matted into their hair. "Yeah," said the younger one, "we musta slid on something and fell because I was unconscious and woke up here and . . ." His voice trailed off.

The older guy asked, "Can you help us? We can't find the road to our car."

"It's right over there," I said. "I just came up that way." It was still too dark under the trees to see the road.

"Over there?" They laughed a little with relief and embarrassment. "It's just been over there? We coulda found it!"

"Hey," I interjected. "How long have you guys been here?"

"Oh, just a . . . I dunno." The old guy turned to his son. "Seems like quite a while, don't it?"

"Maybe a week?" The younger man scratched his head, then looked at his fingers, as if surprised by what came off under his fingernails. Both men were amazingly dirty.

"Well, we can get going later on," said the old guy added happily. "Want some coffee?"

"No, thanks," I said. So they had no clear idea how much time had passed since Danni and I attacked them. And they didn't seem too worried about it, either. I remembered all the missing persons drama after their disappearance, search teams everywhere.

"Well, you guys take care," I said. "I'll just keep on with my walk." As if it was normal to stroll around in the dark.

"You're going to leave? I was just going to fix you some coffee."

"Oh, maybe I'll drop by again," I said. "The road's right there, if you want to find it. I'm going there right now."

I turned my back on them and waded through the grass toward the road. I gave them a goodbye wave before the darkness wrapped around me. They were just staring at me, bewildered. "It's right over here," I called. But the truth was that in the dark I couldn't find the road either.

But I didn't need it to leave. I looked around for Danni and saw her behind me, a swirl of light drifting between the trees. She joined me and we shifted into real time and took to the sky. In real time, the moon had swung over toward the horizon, and the sky was a dark pinkish gray. Maybe two hours had gone by, enough to move from darkness to the first fragile wisps of dawn.

I swam through the ashy air toward their car, an old two-door, still parked on the old logging road. The police had been all over it after their disappearance, but had found no clues. I guess their heirs hadn't wanted it.

Danni and I hovered in the sky. I took a moment to look all around at the miles of dark forest, the patches of clear-cut, and the lakes scattered here and there. It was an illusion of nature.

The reality was that nature was overtaken by fleas and ticks and over-hunting and cycles broken and most of the fairies were dead and gone.

I thought about those guys sitting up there drinking their morning coffee for years. The winters had come and gone, three-wheelers had roared by on the track, probably other hunters had wandered through, and all the while they'd just sat there with their coffee. To them, they'd hardly been there long enough to be worried. I didn't know if they'd experienced a very slow passage of time or if something about fairy time made them just not care.

And I didn't know how I felt about it. Angry. Sad. Glad they weren't dead in a way, but at the same time wanting them *all* to be dead. All the people who fucked up our beautiful world.

Danni flicked her fingers on my arm. She wanted to go home.

I landed with a thud on the pine needles behind my cabin. The sun had popped up over the horizon and the day was starting. I usually like to spend some time with coffee on the porch, watching the mist burn off the lake. My mind doesn't really get working until after I've had that non-thinking-just-staring time.

So I putzed around getting coffee and settled in with my feet up on the railing. Yet the peaceful feeling just wouldn't come. I was tired from getting up early with Danni, and my mind buzzed around in circles, making my head hurt. How much money I had. How much I needed. What I needed to do that day. I kept drinking coffee and going around and around in my mind until it was time to head into town and pick up old lady Allen from her night of carousing with her lover. If that was what she was doing.

I'd been wondering about those hunters every now and again for years. They were the only ones Danni had ever tried to kill. Mostly she glamoured people into getting lost. She'd get them out somewhere surrounded by miles of knee-deep marsh and let the mosquitoes and the weather do the dirty work. But stash someone in fairy time—and just leave them there? It was an interesting idea.

CHAPTER FOURTEEN:

Still Thursday Morning

She was waiting for me out front of the office, clutching her purse with both hands, nice and neat in her low heels and her pink pants and sweater. I pulled up, turned the engine off, and hopped out. She waited for me to open the passenger side door and lowered herself carefully onto the seat.

As usual it was a struggle to get the seatbelt latch hooked in. I tried to make a joke of it but wasn't really in the mood. "Uh, uh, uh," I grunted, "Pushing hard, pushing hard." It was an old joke.

"Oh, you did it! You hit the right spot!" she replied sweetly. That sweet innocent smile. I was so tempted to glamour her then and ask about her tryst. But I didn't. I just shoved the keys in the ignition and got us moving.

We rolled through town at the required twenty-five miles an hour. I could see right away that something was going on; there was a big crowd in front of the county building—Building Number Two, now that the militia was Building Number One. Of course a big crowd for our town wasn't really much of a crowd. The militia was out in force, though, lined up on the steps that led up to the front door.

The county building is the most impressive in town. It's stone, for one thing, big blocks of it. And it's built up over a daylight basement so the front door has to be reached by climbing up a set of stone stairs. The doors are double, though they only open on one side. Inside there's militia guys on duty with metal detectors. For this morning's event, the militia guys were outside flanking the door, and there was a pair on each descending step. It looked like royalty was about to make an appearance, but my guess was the Congressman was going to give a speech.

The crowd was standing around in the grass and on the sidewalk. There weren't enough of them to spill out into the street. Someone had prepped the crowd with red, white, and blue balloons, each with a slogan that I couldn't read but assumed said something about being happy. Over the door two banners had been hung. One said "Freedom" and the other said "From Socialism".

"Do you want to stop?" Mrs. Allen asked. She was leaning toward her window, peering out with an odd expression. Anger?

I didn't want to, but I pulled over on the far side of the street and parked. She smiled, "Yes, we can watch from here! Such a good idea!" Back to that sweet old lady act. She rolled her window down.

A man emerged from the county building. Not the Congressman, just some suit. He had a handheld mike, and he hollered through it at the crowd about what a lovely day it was and how great it was to see everyone. I didn't think the crowd looked all that enthusiastic, in general. There was an amen corner: younger men dressed alike in dark clothes, all wearing dark glasses. Looked like militia wannabes. And scattered around were white men with big guts and worn T-shirts sporting jingoistic slogans. They pumped their fists and yelled off and on.

But even with those isolated displays of enthusiasm, it

wasn't like the crowds back when the coup was underway. Those crowds had been scary: big, solid masses of people, their faces and voices distorted with hate and anger, hollering out group chants about locking people up or killing people. We had rallies like that right here, people who'd known each other for years screaming that their neighbors should be locked up.

But this crowd as a whole wasn't really into it. The others were squinting into the morning sun and waiting for the Congressman.

He appeared a few minutes later, stepped through the doors with both arms raised like he was the Second Coming. Mrs. Allen shifted in her seat. I couldn't see her face.

"Ladies and gentleman," he launched into his speech. I had to admit, he had a very smooth delivery. He didn't peddle the transparent hate that used to be a staple of the party; instead, he was like ice cream: cool and smooth and pleasing. He placed pauses in his speech to give the crowd opportunities to applaud—and got the clapping he wanted.

I couldn't make out more than a phrase or two from his stream of words; there was some distortion in the mike. I heard "freedom" many times, of course, and "end of the welfare state"—that was one of his applause lines, and it got a snort from Mrs. Allen.

Then he talked about "reform" and "free enterprise" and the "value of working" and "freedom to make your own happiness," which got another snort from Mrs. Allen.

He wound up to his closing by exhorting the crowd to ignore the nay-sayers and take his word for it that the economy was great, and we were living in a time of creativity and forward movement; we could all go out and make our own success and be happy. Mrs. Allen's lips were drawn tight across her teeth.

"I am getting the impression that you are not a fan," I said.

"He's a wolf," she answered. She turned to me and said, "There's a Russian proverb, 'Man is wolf to man'. He's a wolf."

I was so surprised that I just stared at her. Then I said, "They're all wolves." I meant not just the Congressman but the party and the donors who owned it and the voters who voted for it.

"Of course they are. Territorial pack-hunting predators. I used to teach history. I can recognize patterns of behavior." Her voice was clipped. Each word snipped out impatiently. I had a sudden memory of her in the classroom, us students thoroughly under control. She'd always been like that: sweet as pie until you crossed her. "Greedy oligarchal predators."

Well, I thought, *now I know where she stands on politics.*

"Have you heard enough?" she asked, her tone indicating that she'd heard more than enough.

"Sure," I said. Then I added, "Let's get on with making ourselves happy." She did that snort again, and we shared a smile.

We didn't talk on the drive home, though I got the feeling of separate intense thinking going on. I was thinking about the Congressman's command of the audience. It was so much like a glamour that I considered the possibility that he might be part fairy.

But it seemed unlikely; that stuff about the Seelie and the Unseelie—the good fairies and the bad ones—is so much hooey. We're all just nature spirits. And even a very old full fairy couldn't glamour a whole crowd.

No, the Congressman was just playing on what Mrs. Allen said about humans as wolves. He was the alpha, and the crowd was the betas and deltas and epsilons, happily making their own happiness by letting him do their thinking for them. And he had another appeal: He led them into believing they were part of something bigger than themselves, heroic participants in a pack drama, their pack against the other packs.

So he was much more powerful than any fairy, especially a halfie like me. I can fly, I can glamour to some extent, and I have a half-assed ability with fairy time and a very limited ability to put people in thrall and that's it. He had the whole power of billionaires behind him and the political party they owned. And they controlled the media and the elections too.

Fairy magic has never been strong compared to human stupidity and greed. And money.

I stared glumly at the passing clear-cuts. Beside me, Mrs. Allen was also staring grimly straight ahead in a way that made me wish fairies could read minds. I wanted to know what she was up to with those strange trips to the motel, and I wanted to know in a way that went beyond my previous curiosity. Like maybe she was part of the Resistance.

There was supposed to be a resistance movement, but I didn't know if it was real or not. The news had stories about ecoterrorists sabotaging timber companies or attacking factory farms. Supposedly someone had released a whole bunch of fur farm foxes down state somewhere. I couldn't see Mrs. Allen doing that.

I could imagine her as part of something political: maybe trying to help . . . I don't know. Help people who were trying to take refuge in Canada? People running from the police? There were supposedly terrorists that were helping Muslims flee the internment camps or escape before getting sent to one. I was well into a fantasy about her heroically leading refugees through frozen marshes on snow shoes in a blizzard when we swung off the highway and into the trailer court.

We rolled past the suspicious children and got some hostile stares from adults and stray dogs, and I pulled up at her pretty flower-bedecked trailer. And I thought: *You are so faking being the respectable little old lady.*

The hell with it. As she handed me my fee, I said in my glamouring voice, "Hey, tell me what you do in that motel room because I'm curious as hell but will never tell anyone else."

Her eyes met mine, and I saw the struggle. I literally could see her face muscles twitching. I pushed harder, but I knew my impulse had been a mistake. I'd been too abrupt. She said stuffily, "I meet an old friend from out of town."

She beat me. She told the truth, but the truth was a lie. She had enough control to beat me. I was kind of embarrassed. She didn't know I was trying to glamour her, but she did know I was prying. She gave me that nail-you-to-the-wall school teacher look and dropped her fee in my lap.

"I can get myself out." And she pushed the car door open and started dragging herself to her feet without me. I got out and ran round to give her my arm anyway. She can fall into the car seat pretty easily but has trouble getting back out of it. After a hesitation, she grabbed my arm, and I helped her up. Then she gathered herself, thanked me very formally, and marched off to her door in a way that said clearly that my escort was not wanted or needed.

I got back in my car, feeling lousy.

I drove off feeling lousy. The truth is I don't glamour people I like very often. I glamour people I don't know or don't like mostly to get them to hurry up and do what they were going to do anyway. Like: "Take my fee and give me the fucking permit."

You have to pay a fee and get a permit for everything these days. Or: "Stop chatting and ring up my groceries." I hate store clerks who chat. And I use the glamour while playing poker to get the players with weak hands to fold so my weak hand can win or to get the marginal ones to be too confident and bet high before I convince them to fold. Mostly I play on feelings that the target has already, like sexual attraction, and just amplify it. I rarely try to make someone do something they just flat out don't want to do.

Well, I tried it with an old lady school teacher who was beginning to trust me, and all I did was piss her off.

Of course that meant she was hiding something, so maybe there *was* a resistance and maybe she was part of it. Intriguing thought.

Back to that trust thing. No one trusts anyone else anymore. You can't. You're either in one of the wolf packs and are always jockeying for position, or you are out of the wolf pack and trying not to get eaten. And nearly everyone is involved in something illegal. You have to be since no one makes enough money to support themselves except the wolves, and they don't obey the law because, as the enforcers, they don't have to. Man is wolf to fucking man.

Meanwhile, I had to go back to town to see Arne. I stopped at the gas station and bamboozled the clerk out of a couple of granola bars and some beer just for the sake of being mean to someone. At least I felt a little better when I drove out to the jail.

Arne didn't look like himself. He was smaller, diminished. It wasn't the lighting, though that was bad enough. The overhead fluorescents made us both look as green as Martians, and his electric orange jumpsuit in the weird harsh light was enough to induce a headache. Arne himself was almost invisible behind his over-bright clothes in the glaring light. He looked like a chewed up piece of jerky.

"Hey," I dropped into my seat and tried to force out some cheerfulness. "I'm making headway on getting you out of here. I have work lined up, and I'm making money." He nodded but without energy. His eyes flicked over my shoulder at the bored militiaman who was leaning against the wall.

"I need you to endorse your check." I shoved it across the table to him. The militia guy watching us snatched up the check, glared at it, and handed it to Arne. Then he said, "Prisoners aren't allowed to have sharp objects."

Arne was so defeated that he didn't even look up. I had to fight an impulse that would've gotten me jailed for sure. Instead I tried glamouring. I looked at the militia guy and said, "It's just his paycheck. Can we borrow a pen for just a moment?"

I could feel the thoughts wiggling around in his head, and I think he might have agreed if he'd had a pen in his pocket, but he didn't. So he shook his head at us, his lips tight.

"Never mind." I turned back to Arne. "It's one twenty-five a day, I hear. I'm shooting for Monday. I'll have the money by then."

He nodded glumly.

"So how are you? How's the food? At that price, the food ought to be pretty good."

He lifted one shoulder. "Food comes from the diner, so it's good. Everything's ok. Except that old lady who never stops crying."

Then he met my eyes. "How's Poochie?"

"Mean as ever," I told him. Arne cracked a grin. "So he's okay. Slept in my bed last night. Probably pooping on the floor as we speak."

Arne sighed. "That old lady never stops crying about her dog. Do you think you could . . . maybe go get the dog or something?"

I hunched my shoulders. As if I didn't have enough on my plate. "What old lady?"

"I don't know. She's two doors down, but I can hear her. She's been in for a month, she says, and her dog got left and no one is taking care of it."

I felt a stab in my gut. Probably dead by now. "What's her name?"

"She says it's Ratko. Does that sound right to you? Mavis Ratko."

"Maybe Polish? Did she say where she lives?"

"No. I shoulda asked." Arne shrugged helplessly.

"Hey, no problem! I'll figure it out. Town this size can't have too many names like that in the phone book. And you'll be out by Monday, okay? So just hang in there."

As I drove away, my slow burn turned into a one-man forest fire. I was still planning on getting the money, but not on Sunday. I was working up a different plan for sooner than that.

CHAPTER FIFTEEN:

thursday Night

I followed Danni at a distance. I could see her in the night air as a transparent sheen, a mist over the stars, an iridescent glitter in the edge of my eye. We sailed through the night sky, high over the black trees and the silvery lakes. I didn't know where she was going, but she was headed somewhere. She was looking for something.

I knew I was dreaming because I wasn't cold. The night air in the late summer has a real snap to it and, if you add wind chill, it's really fucking cold for the warm-blooded. But I wasn't feeling anything at all.

Besides, my point of view kept shifting. I saw the dark blue shadows on the snow from above, as if I was an owl flying through the treetops. I saw the scratchy, witchy fingers of the pines from amongst the trees as if I was a squirrel. I saw the wet, black tree trunks from snow level as if I was a winter hare, crouching in the dark, afraid. I even saw the nighttime through Danni's eyes as she wended her way between the upper branches of the trees, slipping in and out of moon shadow, visible only as a glimpse of glittery reflected moonlight. Visible to me because once again, I was seeing her with my dreamer's eyes. I knew I was not going to lose track of her. I was drawn to follow.

Then I saw her slide down into the darkness of the underbrush, into the dense, wet, cold region of crisscrossed branches burdened with snow. I followed, twisting between the branches, never touching the snow because it was a dream and I wasn't really there.

Then suddenly I found myself hovering over a small meadow by a stream. I was reminded of the old days: huge, silently watchful trees; clear, cold, tea-colored water; a marshy stream lined with lush grasses and sedges. The snow was gone, replaced by the warm, richly scented darkness of summer. The air was full of fireflies, and the black sky was glittery with stars. I was stabbed by an intense nostalgia for my childhood, for the time spent playing outside after dark with Danni. She used to take me on flying adventures through the trees and meadows and lakes, looking for animals, while she taught me about their lives and struggles: the secret lives of moose, foxes, wolverines, loons.

I became aware of a dark shape in the long lush grass: a mother moose, followed by her gangly calf. For one sweetly intense moment I forgot I was dreaming and thought I was actually a kid again out in the woods with Danni. But no, the mother moose was one of the few remaining survivors. I could tell because her coat was ragged from the fleas, and she looked underfed. *She must be lonely,* I thought. Her movements were heavy and sad. The wobbly calf trailed along behind her. What future was there for her baby?

I realized then that there was something wrong with the calf. It was skinny, and its head hung heavy on its frail neck. I watched as its fur peeled back, exposing red flesh that oozed with the yellow goo of infection. Skinny trembling legs could barely hold the calf upright. Even in the dark, I could see that the calf was dying, and I could feel its fear and despair. The mother waited in the meadow as the calf struggled through the long grass to her side.

I knew what was wrong—the warm winters weren't

killing fleas. The flea population had exploded and the weaker fur-bearing animals of every kind were being sucked dry of blood. The calf staggered through the meadow grass and stopped, swaying on its shaky stick legs. Then it fell into a little heap of bones and raggedy fur, barely visible in the deep grass. Its mother nuzzled it with her nose, but the calf did not rise.

Danni swam through the air over the meadow. She was as bright as the fireflies, a swirl of shiny colors. She went to the mother first and laid her head on the cow's broad, dark shoulder. Together they sniffed the calf and licked it. Then Danni slid down the mother's side and lay down in the grass with the calf. She curled around its boney body, cradled its head in her arms, and rested her head against its cheek. I watched as her light dimmed and flickered out, and she too was gone.

The mother moose and I stared at the scene before us. I don't think either of us understood what had happened. The moose shoved her nose against the calf and tried to wake it, but it lay still. She tried poking the calf with one hoof and tried pushing it again with her nose. Then she stepped back and stared up at the sky.

It seemed like every star in the universe was shining that night with no obscuring haze of smoke. I could see Orion and the Dipper and Cassiopeia and others, even constellations that didn't belong in an August sky. The stars weren't crying, just watching. They offered no comfort except an awareness of vast expanses of distance and time, an infinite universe, cycles beyond our knowledge. Then the mother moose turned away from her baby and slowly, awkwardly stumbled into the forest and disappeared into the darkness.

CHAPTER SIXTEEN:

Friday Morning

I woke up slowly, heavy with knowledge. Poochie stirred but not irritably. He seemed depressed, too, probably missing Arne. I got up and threw on some clothes, picked up Poochie, and left.

I walked up to Sally's cabin, lead-footed: Danni was gone, I felt it. I would never see my friend again. Sally was up, sitting at her table with a cup of coffee, Charlie by her side holding his tea. She glanced up at me as I came in and wiped a tear on her sleeve. Charlie gave her shoulder a little pat and, with great weariness, she leaned into him and rested her head against his chest. I set Poochie down and sat across from them. Sally's eyes were closed. Charlie stared at the tabletop. His fingers fondled her hair.

No one said anything. After a few moments, Sally sat up, wiped her face again, and whispered hoarsely, "Want some breakfast?"

"You sit there," I said. "I'll fix something for you." I climbed to my feet. I moved carefully, as if my chest was full of nitroglycerin.

"I'm not really hungry." Sally sighed and rubbed her eyes. Her hair was an uncombed mess, and her eyes were red.

"I know," I said. "But we are still alive, and we have to

keep on going." And I had to keep that nitro balanced and stable.

I fixed blueberry pancakes for all of us and gave Poochie some of the dried trout Sally stores up for winter.

Then I told them my plan.

The Walmart in Ste. Abelle sold burner cell phones. I didn't buy one, of course. I just walked out with it. I sat in the car and fiddled around with it until I got service, and then I drove back home.

Since I had the rest of the day to kill, I got the phone book from Sally and read through the R's. No Ratko, but there was a Rathko. I dialed and got a 'no longer in service' message. I wrote down the address and headed out.

I felt like I was burning up a lot of my life driving back and forth to Bear Lake. Usually I don't go to town unless it's for a job with Arne and that's usually just in spurts of a day or two, followed by a week of being at home. I don't like being in town—too much time away from the lake and the trees gets on my nerves.

I flipped off the Report Aliens sign as I passed it by and flipped off the gun shop too. But I checked first to make sure no one could see me.

Then I turned off Main Street and got on one of the back streets that runs parallel and cruised along slowly, reading street signs. Mrs. Rathko's house was on Pine, the third street. I turned onto Pine and started counting down addresses. Her house was easy to spot; there was a sign out front that said it was up for auction by the county. I parked and got out.

It was a little cottage in a neighborhood of little cottages:

vintage working class housing. Her house should've been cute; there was a front porch surrounded by flowerbeds and some kind of vine growing over the picket fence. But the lawn wasn't mowed, the flowerbeds were spiky with dead stems and leaves, and the house itself seemed to be crouching in despair: the windows dark, newspapers piled up at the front door.

I opened the gate and started up the front walk. A feeling of dread filled my stomach. A heavy, thick silence surrounded the house; no dog barked at my approach.

Since I was going to break in, I went around to the back. I more or less had permission—since Arne had sent me on this quest to help out the old lady—so I wasn't being sneaky exactly, but I didn't want a neighbor calling the militia, either. Mrs. Rathko's backyard was set up for a dog: safely fenced, with a dog bed and accompanying bowls on the back porch. Still no barking. I listened to the silence, depressed.

Then I jumped a mile, startled, when a voice reached me from over the fence: a woman in the back yard next door. She was a squat little figure under a huge sun hat, standing next to her mulch pile with gardening shears in her hands. She had a beat up face and bad teeth, but her eyes were kind.

"Hello?" she called. "Are you a friend of Mavis's?"

I walked over to the fence, and she joined me on the other side. "I don't know her, but she's a friend of a friend. I came to check on her dog."

"Oh, I am so glad!" She broke out a big smile, then leaned in toward me and whispered, "I've been feeding her secretly."

"Secretly?"

"Yeah, the county, you know, they took Mavis's house. So I didn't want anyone to know I was going in and out."

She grimaced with embarrassment. "I broke a window." Her hand went up to her mouth, a shy gesture.

So I didn't need to break in because she already had. I grinned my approval, but she didn't smile back.

"But that dog is so lonely over there that it just breaks my heart. And I can't keep her because I rent." She was blinking back tears. "Mavis and I have been neighbors for years, and I can remember that dog from being a pup. She's a nice little dog."

"I'll take her," I heard myself say. Another dog. Sally would be pissed. Oh, well.

"Oh, thank you Jesus!" She actually clasped her hands in prayer. I thought: *What does Jesus have to do with this?* But I didn't say anything aloud, not even when she went on to chant, "Praise the Lord! Praise the Lord." I just started walking toward the back porch.

She called out, all excited, "I'll be right with you," and bustled along the fence to her front yard, cut around the corner, and arrived in Mavis's backyard out of breath but alit with smiles.

We didn't have to go into the house to get the dog; she ran out the minute the door opened and leaped joyfully into Neighbor Lady's arms. Another little white dog for our collection. This one was frantically friendly and kept wriggling and twisting so that Neighbor Lady had a hard time hanging on to her.

Neighbor Lady handed the squirmy little body over to me. Then she got very serious, leaned in, and whispered, "God bless you." I must've looked skeptical, because she nodded firmly and stated as a fact, "You will be redeemed on Judgment Day and it's coming. You know how the Book says fire next time?"

I nodded.

"Well, it is fire," she said, "just like prophecy. And most people will get what they deserve. It's the animals I feel sorry for."

"Yeah, me too," I muttered, backing away from her. I was in complete agreement about the animals, but I didn't like the fervency in her eyes: too sad and scared. She was like someone hanging on the edge of a deep well by her fingertips, and she was getting teary. I wanted to escape, so I mumbled, "God bless you too." Then I retreated into Mrs. Rathko's side yard, calling over my shoulder, "I'll take good care of the dog."

Neighbor Lady followed me around to the front yard, trotting along as I hustled with the wiggling dog clutched to my chest. I flung the dog into the car and closed the door. My last sight of Neighbor Lady was her squat figure coming out into the street to wave goodbye.

Sally frowned, "Another dog?"

Charlie said, "He's cute."

"He's a she," I responded. "Look underneath."

"Okay." Sally banged dishes together in the sink. That's how she shows disapproval: noisy housework. "*She*'s another dog. At this rate, the dogs will soon outnumber us."

Charlie had the look of a disappointed child. I almost expected him to start whining "Please, please, please" at Sally.

"And that other dog, that little rat dog, bites." Sally glared at me.

I objected, "He can't bite. He hasn't got any teeth."

"Well, he tries to. It's the thought that counts."

I pondered that, then argued, "No it isn't. It's actions that speak louder than words, and he gums people. He might want to bite but he—"

"Oh, for crying out loud!" Sally screamed. Charlie and I stared at her open mouthed. "Okay, keep the damn dog, but can I at least be asked before you bring home the next one?"

"Sure," I said. "I mean there won't be a next one." Sally turned her back on us, but I could tell she was crying. Charlie and I exchanged looks. I realized, then, that this drama was not about the dog. I'm slow on the uptake sometimes, I guess.

I spent the rest of the day putzing around the place, fixing things and cleaning things—anything to keep my mind occupied. I guess we were all coping with Danni's death in our own way, my way being to focus the front part of my mind on keeping busy and the back part on my plan. I swept the sticks and pine needles off the porches. Got the ladder out and attacked the grunge in the gutters. I was so burning with energy that I just couldn't stop. I even went into my cabin with a broom and dustpan.

We didn't have dinner together. I guess Sally couldn't face a family meal with Danni missing. I wasn't hungry anyway. When it finally got dark, we sat on Sally's porch and shared a bottle of some kind of red wine. I didn't drink much of it. I was just trying to fill the time.

Sally had recovered from her crying jag and made me go over the plan while we tried to find holes in it. We discussed the timing, the logistics, the way things could go wrong, and what we would do if it all went pear-shaped. We watched the darkness settle into the forest, watched the moon shining fuzzily through the hazy sky, watched the fireflies dancing over the lake. Sally and Charlie sedated themselves with booze while I got myself wound up tighter and tighter. Then finally, finally, finally it was time.

I flew away over our forest and out a couple miles across clear-cuts to a random place in the darkness. Then I checked Charlie's watch which I had borrowed since I don't have one: 11 p.m. I phoned the Congressman.

He answered on the third ring, "Yup?" I could hear voices and light music, like a cocktail party, maybe.

"Hey," I said, trying to sound businesslike. "Are you still interested in a bear?"

"Yeah, sure." His voice rose. "Can you get us one?"

Okay, good. "Yeah, but you guys have to move fast. I mean right now."

"We can do that." He got all excited. "Is it a big one?" Asshole. There were no bears, big or otherwise. "Yep," I said. "Big male. Huge. But be quiet. Are you at a party?"

"No, just a few people. Friends. I stepped outside so they can't hear us."

"Well, don't tell them about the bear. Tell them you have to go deal with something political, something . . . where are you?"

"I'm at a restaurant."

"Tell them there's someone you have to talk to confidentially, so you have to leave."

"That'll work," he said briskly. "Okay, we're on our way. Where should we meet you?"

"Just get your guys and drive south out of town. Be sure to mind the speed limit."

He laughed.

"No seriously," I said. "We don't want to attract any attention. I don't want any attention." The militia wouldn't give him a ticket. I just didn't want him to tell anyone that he was meeting me because he'd shoot off his mouth for sure if he got stopped for speeding.

"Okay, so drive south. Check your odometer. Start looking for me about nine miles south of town. Look to your right just after the bridge. There's a gravel road there. Get your guys and get moving because I have the bear baited, but he won't stick around forever." I didn't have to fake urgency in my voice. I felt prickly, as if my body was full of static electricity.

"Can do!" He hung up.

I clicked off the phone. Then I landed down in the field of stumps and brush and dismantled the cell phone. Using my headlamp, I hunted around until I found a couple of rocks. I bashed the sim card and the phone to bits. Then I took off and flew back toward home.

I landed by the trapper's car on the old logging road that runs along the edge of our woods. The darkness fell around me, a soft, comforting blanket of secrecy. The forest was full of smells: water, tannins, pines, rot, and growth. I could smell the dusty gravel road too.

I could see almost nothing, just variations on the absence of light: midnight blue sky, silhouetted black trees, the impenetrable darkness of the underbrush. And I could hear almost nothing: just a sigh of breeze, the soft crunch of gravel as I shifted my feet, and my own breath.

But I was so full of adrenaline that I couldn't just stand around waiting. I clicked on my headlamp and stomped down the gravel road to the pavement. I took a quick look at the darkness—no cars coming—and stomped back up to the trappers' derelict car. Then I walked around, staring at the harsh yellow spot my headlamp made on the ground, wandered back down to the pavement, back up the road and around again. I kept checking Charlie's watch, micro-monitoring the passage of seconds. How long would it take for the Congressman to round up the Russians, get their guns, pile them all into a car, and drive down here? Only about nine miles, so not much drive time. Twenty minutes?

I made the short trek down to the pavement again and, poised on the edge of the gravel, I bounced on my feet—heel, toe, heel, toe—like a little kid who needed the toilet. I told myself over and over to cut it out, but I couldn't calm down.

I knew why I was so wound up. We didn't take major action against people much. We didn't want the fallout, the flapdoodle afterwards. Humans let each other die of starvation or disease, they let each other die of drugs or neglect, they let each other die of loneliness—unknown and unmourned until the stink of rot gets noticeable and finally the authorities are called—but, shit, let one hunter go missing, and the search parties are out stomping all over the woods for weeks. A Congressman goes missing? The militia would be hysterical. Completely frickin' hysterical. So that's what I was so wound up about—the aftermath.

I just wanted to get it over with. And with that thought, a pair of yellow lights stabbed my eyes, followed by the grinding thrum of an engine, harsh against the soft darkness. I flicked off my headlamp and retreated back up the gravel road in case it wasn't them.

I kept out of sight until I saw the headlights swing as the car pulled over. Then I took a deep breath and strolled down toward them. One of the Russians rolled a window down and called, "Mr. Fallon?"

"Yep. This is the place." I made my voice laconic. In

fact, I lapsed into the stereotype of the backwoods redneck they thought I was. I watched them pile out of the car, silhouetted by the interior light. The doors slammed, the light went out, and the guys bunched up in the dark, joking and laughing and clicking on their flashlights.

I said, "Hey, make some more noise, why dontcha. That bear wants company."

The Congressman hissed, "Quiet down, everybody." They all had great big guns and were grinning ear to ear. "So where's this bear?" the Congressman asked.

"This way and be quiet." I said. I wanted to get them away from the highway before someone drove by and saw all the lights, so I walked ahead, guiding them up the old road. "I set the bait up the trail a little ways," I whispered. I kept them moving past the old car—which excited a lot of whispered comment and guys telling each other to hush up—and we finally arrived up around the corner where the road narrowed into a trail. There I stopped and waited. They all stopped, too, bouncing on their toes and milling around impatiently. There was a pause before the Congressman figured it out.

"Oh, sure, five up front, was it?"

"It was one thousand up front," I said. I was glamouring as hard as I could. I saw the reluctance in his fingers as he thumbed through the bills. He was wondering if he'd really promised that much up front. But he didn't want to argue then and there. Besides, throwing money around made him feel big in front of the Russians.

He peeled off the bills with a flourish. I counted the money in the light of my headlamp. I tried to think of some way to get the rest of his money, but, with all those guns around, I didn't want to take the chance.

Well, I just wasn't going to get more, that's all. I shoved

the money into my back pocket and said, "We have to keep quiet now." I scanned with the headlamp, found the trail, and started walking. They followed, trying to be quiet.

I shifted us into fairy time. I felt the lurch, but no one else seemed to notice, maybe because we all felt a little off-kilter anyway from walking in the dark. The flash lit the ground with a hard yellow light that illuminated only the trail immediately in front of me. I was very aware of the night smells and the quiet tramping of feet. I heard the occasional mutter of anticipation, muted laughter, and a curse or two when someone stumbled. The men could turn down their volume but couldn't shut themselves up completely, I guess. It seemed like the trail went on and on and on before we finally saw the glimpse of campfire.

"Is that a fire?" the Congressman whispered. "Who's over there?"

"Just some guys I know. Trappers. Real bear hunters."

Using the fire as a guide, we thrashed our way through branches and ferns. I heard the Russians behind me complaining and grumbling as we stumbled through the underbrush. The trappers heard us coming and stood up. I could see that one still had a cup of coffee. "Hey, hello," I called softly.

"Who are you?" the young man yelled. His voice was shrill with fear.

"Tell them quiet!" barked one of the Russians.

"It's just me," I said. We fought our way clear of the underbrush and emerged into the long grass of the little meadow where the walking was easier. The young man and his dad stood shoulder to shoulder, watching us approach. As we got closer, I could see that they were in rough shape, really dirty, the dried blood on their heads visible as black stains in the light of the flashlights.

The Congressman got spooked. "What's going on here?" he demanded. "Who are these guys?"

"Well, who the hell are *you*?" the young guy shot back.

"Hey, calm down, everyone," I snarled. I pointed at the two trappers and said, "These two guys are trappers." Then I pointed at the Congressman and said, "This is Congressman Van Dusen, and these are the guys who own him. You all might as well sit down and get acquainted because you're going to be here awhile."

Everyone started yelling questions at me then, so I shifted back to regular time, jumped into the sky, and left.

Back in real time, it was that dark gray period of very early morning before the sun peeks out. I could see the clearing below me and the dense dark forest around it. Farther away, I could see miles of clear-cut and the acres of second and third growth timber. The darkness smoothed away the damage and created a pattern of textures in tones from slate to coal to the darkest of forest green.

I wondered what the Congressman was saying to the trappers and the trappers to him. It was still dark where they were. At the rate they were going, it would be a year of real time before they got done shouting questions at each other and sat down. Meanwhile, I had a thousand dollars of cash in my pocket. But I had to cover up all the evidence, and that was going to take a while.

I flew back to their car, burning with energy and, yeah, fear. They'd locked it up, and I thought about how mad Arne would be if he could see what I was going to do with that car. Arne loves cars. *Too bad I can't steal it for him,* I thought. It was a shiny, polished, leather-seated, over-priced piece of vainglory, a wet dream. Yeah, too bad.

I got a big rock and bounced it off the back window, making a mess of spider web cracks. Then I bounced it some more and some of the cracks widened and split. With my third blow, the window shattered into chunks. I climbed up on the trunk and crawled head first onto the back seat. It was awkward as hell but eventually I floundered my way into the front seat. I stuck my head under the dash and fiddled around with the screwdriver I'd brought along in my back pocket.

My dad taught me how to hotwire cars. It isn't hard.

It was still probably no later than six, still early for people to be driving into town. I checked for traffic and saw no one. I drove south about ten miles and started looking for the turn off to the old abandoned gravel pit. And there it was: a dirt road leading off through the stunted messy growth of a clear-cut. The pit itself filled with water in the spring but was bone dry in the late summer. I stopped in the middle of the parking area, well away from the straggly plant life around the edges. Then I filled the interior of the car with twigs, thin dry branches, and dry leaves, and used Charlie's lighter to set it on fire.

I skimmed low to the treetops on the way back. The first firetruck was whizzing by about the time I got to the old logging road where the trappers' car was parked. I got a branch and swept all the footprints and car tracks away. It's a good thing Charlie watches cop shows on his computer; I don't think I would've thought of all of this without his advice.

I lumbered into the sky and took off for home, so weary my body felt like a rag. I watched the trees of our forest pass below me. The deciduous trees were beginning to lose their greenery and the pines and firs were darkening. I felt the first shivers of winter in the air. To my mild surprise, there were clouds piling up in the north. Maybe we would finally receive the blessing of a rain.

CHAPTER SEVENTEEN:

Saturday Morning

I landed on Sally's porch with a bump and a lurch and staggered over to a chair where I collapsed like an empty sack. I felt no satisfaction. Not the money wadded up in my pocket, not even the thought of springing Arne gave me any excitement. I felt completely empty.

Sally and Charlie emerged quietly from the cabin, each with a dog. They looked hung over. Poochie scrambled out of Sally's arms and jumped into my lap. I summoned up the energy to give him a pat.

Sally settled on the railing, silhouetted against the morning light. We were going to have another smoky day. In fact, the smoke was worse. The car fire? I didn't think it could spread to the trees—not from a gravel pit.

"So how'd it go?" She asked.

"It went."

She nodded. Charlie clutched his dog and looked worried. I closed my eyes.

Sally brought me some coffee and one of her blueberry muffins. She and Charlie chatted for a bit while I slumped there, outwardly resting and inwardly replaying the events of the night with various horror show endings. My mind kept grinding out lurid scenarios: The car fire spread and burnt a thousand acres, the Russians went nuts and shot everyone, a shit load of FBI agents surrounded our cabins and threatened to shoot us all, the money had dropped out of my pocket out over a clear-cut where I'd never find it. I kept making a success into a failure.

Because just leaving them there didn't make up for Danni dying.

Finally Sally and Charlie drifted off, and I gave up on napping. Instead I stumbled blearily down to my cabin and took a shower. Then I drank several cups of coffee and headed into town again with the money. I told Poochie before I left, "Your pal's coming home." He was busy eating a sock and paid no attention.

The coffee had been a bad idea; I was awake but as growly as a bear. Nervy. Everything pissing me off. I knew Arne would be glad to see Poochie again and glad to get back to his filthy dump of a trailer and sleep on his own sweaty sheets, but I couldn't summon up any feelings of happiness or relief. I just felt really, really irritated by absolutely everything.

I drove past the fear-of-aliens billboard, past the gun shop, and on into town. I tried to park in front of Building Number One, but the parking places were marked off limits by orange cones. Oh, I forgot the parade. The stupid parade for the Congressman—oops, no Congressman to lead it! I tried to not think about that. I had to act like I had no idea the Congressman was missing. *Just be normal*, I told myself. What was normal for me? *Okay, be pissed off and exhausted and impatient.*

So I strode around to the front of the building, thinking pissy thoughts about fires and famine and death, but not thinking about a missing Congressman. I shoved the door open and took the three strides necessary to reach the clerk's counter. A different woman was sitting there, this one with a peeved expression behind too much make-up. She looked like an aging biker chick: thin in a too-tight uniform shirt, with an ugly tattoo lurking on her scalp just behind her bleached out hair. She was glaring at the computer, red fingernails poised over the keyboard. She didn't look up.

I leaned against the counter and glared. She pursed her lips and made stabbing motions, muttered and stabbed some more. I said, "Excuse me?"

"We're not open," she snarled without even glancing at me.

"What?" That was not the reaction I had expected. "The doors are open. And the police *can't* be closed. What if someone wants to report a crime?" My voice was shrill with disbelief.

"Are you reporting a crime?" She kept her eyes on the screen. Whatever she saw there was far more annoying to her than me.

"No, I came—"

"Then we're closed. Everyone's out supervising the parade and doing traffic and crowd control."

Crowd control? Bear Lake wasn't big enough to have a crowd, even if the whole fucking town showed up at once.

"I came to pay my friend's fine and get him out of jail." I bit off each word for emphasis and backed it with glamour. "You need to go get him for me."

She finally looked at me, unmoved by my weak, tired-ass attempt at glamour. "I'm sorry, but we ARE closed. I'm just trying to get some data entry done. I'm not really official, just part time helping out." She had one of those mask-like faces. "And there's no one here to go get your friend because, like I said, they are all out supervising the parade."

I took a deep breath. "You can't do it?"

"No, I'm not authorized. You'll have to come back during office hours on Monday."

I imagined grabbing her by the neck and screaming at her until she gave in. I imaged her face smashed in, blood everywhere, my knuckles bruised. I knew how good that would feel. But I couldn't get Arne out of jail that way, and I didn't want to start a manhunt for the two of us. Besides, there was another way to get even.

"The whole militia is out at the parade?"

"Yeah, just about. Sorry."

Stepping back carefully and slowly, I said, "Okay, thank you for your help."

"Sure, sorry." She stabbed the keyboard and glared at the screen.

I walked back to the car with the steady pace of a robot. The caffeine was rocketing up and down my nervous system like fireworks. I could almost feel sparks shooting out my fingertips. But I kept the energy contained, and I drove back to the gun shop slowly, a couple miles per hour under the speed limit, my eyes out for militia. There was plenty of traffic on the way into town, but I was the only one headed out.

She'd said that everyone was in town at the parade and, sure enough, there was only one car there at the gun shop. Just one staffer on duty. I parked around back.

I'd made a decision without telling myself what the decision was. As I approached the door, I pulled my shirt sleeve down over my hand like a glove, so my fingers wouldn't touch the handle. The interior was dark with a long wooden display rack on one side and posters everywhere of guys holding guns—dressed in black—and gals holding guns, hardly dressed at all. Lots of boobs.

Behind the counter slouched a stocky guy with a thin veneer of fuzz on top of his head and a huge, hairy matt of hair hanging off his chin. He had small eyes embedded in a face enlarged by fat. His eyes lit up at the sight of me, a customer, a break in the boredom.

"Hey, hello, how're you doing?" he asked, friendly.

"Oh, pretty good," I spoke casually while I surveyed the wall of guns behind him.

"Going to the parade today?" he asked. "Starts in about half an hour."

"Yeah, wouldn't miss it," I said. "But I thought I'd stop by here on the way in. I need a gun."

"Looking for anything in particular?"

"Yeah, I want a .357 Ruger single shot." How come I was so particular is that's the kind of gun my dad had. We didn't have it anymore because my mom threw it in the lake years ago. One of their disagreements.

"Well, I can help you with that." He moved down the counter, checking the display as he went. At the far end he extracted a large pistol, rolled the barrel to check for the absence of ammo, and brought the gun back to me. "Hefty pistol," he commented. "People can see you have it. And it won't jam."

"Yeah, that's the idea." The .357 Ruger looked like a prop for a cowboy movie. It was designed to shoot one bullet at a time, old style. "I need a box of cartridges." I added. Then I shifted us into fairy time. The militia man swayed a bit and grabbed the counter. Then he laughed, "Ooh, felt weird for a moment. Now what did you want? Shells, was it?"

"Yeah."

"Okey dokey." He dug around behind the counter and handed me a small box. I shook out some shells. Then I released the cylinder and set one in the chamber. And then I closed the gun up and aimed it at his chest.

"Hey, now wait," he said.

Then I shot him.

CHAPTER EIGHTEEN:

Saturday, Later

The parade was late, and I could tell that the townsfolk were getting restless. Small knots of people hung out along the street—not enough for a continuous crowd, but a group here and there with spaces in between. They had come to enjoy the parade and were carrying flags and balloons and signs that said things like: "Welcome Congressman Van Dusen", or "We Love Privatecare". Privatecare was the new thing, a replacement for the old Medicare. Didn't affect me; I don't get human diseases. I was just there establishing an alibi in case I got questioned later. Where was I when the gunshop got robbed? At the parade.

The parade that was missing its focal politician. I was responsible for that too. I moseyed along the sidewalk, trying to fit in and look casual, all the while dodging stray toddlers and meandering old people.

The sight of Building Number Two, the county court house, brought me to a stop. Militiamen were arrayed on the stone steps, three on each side, standing military style with their feet apart and hands behind their backs, all wearing dark glasses. At the top of the steps, the chief of the militia was beginning to fidget. He stood ramrod straight by the door, as if about to salute, but he was rising up and down on his toes slightly and kept shooting side glances down the street.

He shared space at the top of the steps with the mayor, a grayish man who always looks like he's trying to be more important than he actually is. I'd heard he was a substitute teacher in his real life. He was craning his neck, looking up the street anxiously.

I looked around, wondering when the penny would drop. Some kids ran out into the street and their parents hollered at them to get back. They did. Slowly. An old man stepped out, took a long, searching look down the street, and retreated. I saw him shaking his head in response to a question from his wife. Nope, no sign of the parade.

I kept telling myself to calm down, but I was so wired I felt like my bones and nerves were exposed. A dog barked and I jumped. I couldn't hold still, kept shoving my hands in and out of my pockets. I kept telling myself: *You got clean away with it. No one will know.*

But I knew. *All the blood, everything—stop. Don't think about it. Just think about the money.* I'd cleaned out the cash register and walked off with a locked metal box which I hoped would come through with even more cash once I had the time and privacy to open it.

So I had Arne's money plus some. *Fuck you, militia, I'm making my own goddamn happiness.* Defiantly, I surveyed the street. *And pretty soon you'll find out your goddamn Congressman is gone, and I will be even happier yet.* That's when I caught sight of Taylor.

She was across the street and down a little ways, standing with her child. She was one of the few that didn't seem anxious for the parade to start. She had her arms wrapped around herself protectively and looked very tired. Beside her, the little boy was bouncing on his toes and flapping his fingers repetitively. People strolled by, even other kids, but he just kept bouncing and flapping. For the first time, it occurred to me that he might have some kind of mental condition that people get.

I stepped off the curb and crossed the street. As soon as I got in hailing distance, I waved and caught Taylor's attention. A big wide smile lit her face, and she waved back. The boy kept bouncing.

"Hey, how are you," I greeted her. Her smile was too big, too welcoming. I thought: *If I was a wolf, I'd eat you.* But I'm not a wolf. So I just said, "You got a day off?"

"Oh, not usually. Saturday is usually one of the busier days, but I asked if I could take Bryan to the parade. If there is one." She placed her hand on the little boy's head and gently brought his bouncing to an end. "Bryan, this is Mr. Fallon. Say, 'Hello, Mr. Fallon'."

He rolled his big brown eyes in my direction but didn't quite connect. "Hello, Bryan," I said.

"Say hello to Mr. Fallon," Taylor instructed. She had to repeat herself several times before he babbled "Ellomisterfallon" and pulled away. She smiled, a bit embarrassed. "He's got autism." Bryan was on his toes bouncing and flapping again. "This is just his way."

"He looks happy," I said. "Maybe we should all be jumping around." But I didn't mean it. I felt brittle and frail, like a loud noise would break me. Taylor must have sensed something wrong because she asked with real concern, "Are you okay?"

"Yeah, sure, of course." I struggled for an explanation, "I'm just bummed because Arne's still in jail. Kind of clashes with all this celebration."

She grinned ironically. "All this *supposed* to be celebration."

I wasn't sure what she meant by that. Like maybe she

was hinting that she didn't think there was anything to celebrate? Or maybe she was just referring to how late the parade was. So I just said, "Yeah, it's weird to be so late."

That's when a voice on a bullhorn interrupted us. The militia chief, his voice distorted and abrasive, blared out, "Well, folks, I have an unfortunate announcement to make. Our guest of honor, Congressman Van Dusan, has been delayed and so will not be leading our parade." He paused to get everyone's attention. "But that doesn't mean we can't celebrate making our own happiness through our productivity right here in Bear Lake! So the parade will begin shortly, and thank you all for coming to our event. Let's all give a loud cheer for our school marching band as they come into view!"

All around us people began to clap and cheer. Little Bryan responded with a cheer of his own invention: an odd buzzing through his front teeth. Taylor grinned. She corralled his hands and showed him how to clap. Bryan loved that. He incorporated the clapping into his jumping and buzzing.

The marching band hove into view in bright red and blue uniforms, playing "Stars and Stripes Forever". It seemed an odd choice to me, but an awful lot of Bear Lake civic behavior strikes me as odd. I thought the whole idea of a parade was strange, especially one to celebrate the end of government health insurance.

Taylor squinted at the approaching band. "They're not in sync," she commented. "I don't really like parades that much, but it's a chance for Bryan to get out around people. He needs socialization." She looked apologetic.

"He's having a good time," I said. "I think." He'd started whirling in place, and I wondered how long he would be able to keep his balance.

"Yeah, I think he is, if he doesn't get over-excited." She reached for Bryan's shoulder and gently stopped the whirling. Bryan didn't make eye contact with her. I realized that he never did. Her hand was gentle and loving on his shoulder.

"Hey," I said on impulse, "Would you two like to come out to the lake? I live on a small lake," I explained. "It's more of a real lake than Lake Bear."

I don't know where that impulse came from. Maybe it was her hand on her child's shoulder. Maybe it was because I thought Bryan might like the lake. Maybe it was because I was trying to use a pose of casual flirtation to cover the lightening bolts of adrenaline shooting through my arms and legs. Maybe I was trying to act normal because I didn't feel normal.

Then I remembered that I was supposed to be expecting to meet the Congressman and another lightening bolt shot through me. I added hurriedly, "I mean the Congressman is supposed to come out fishing tomorrow morning, but I have the afternoon free so...we could go fishing or go out in the canoe. If you think that would be safe for Bryan, I mean." *Shut up*, I told myself. *You're babbling.*

But she was smiling. "That sounds like fun. Can Bryan swim there? He loves swimming."

I felt a stab of guilt, then, like I didn't have any right to be friends with her and the child. I kept seeing the gun. I'd stashed it under a rock in a stream that flows through a clear-cut. No fisherman will find it because the clear-cut ruined the fishing. Still the gun was taunting me, like it was calling, "I'm here, I'm here."

I should've left it in fairy time with the dead guy, but I was so rattled that I'd shoved it down the back of my pants like guys do in action movies. Cops and criminals do that to have their hands free, at least in fiction. It hadn't worked for me. I got only about halfway to the front door when the damn thing started crawling up my butt, shifting around back there like it was about to fall out. You never see anyone in a movie have their gun fall down their pant leg or fall out the back of their pants. So I managed to get the door open while holding the heavy box and got around to the back of the shop all in fairy time by sort of crab-walking with my butt stuck out to keep the damn gun from falling out. Then I jumped back to real time and threw the gun into the car.

So I just hadn't been thinking. I'd been freaked out. Panicked.

"Bob?" Her eyes were full of worry. "Are you too upset about your friend to entertain guests? Because maybe we could come out some other day?"

I snapped my attention back to her. "Oh, no, come on out. It'll take my mind off Arne." Not that I had been thinking about him.

The band reached us in all their brassy glory, teenagers stomping along slightly out of time with each other but bravely hooting and tooting and drumming. We applauded along with the rest of the crowd. Then we kept on clapping for a couple of floats, some baton twirlers, a bunch of people in identical jackets who were riding horses, and a bunch of Ford Novas—God knows what that was all about.

Next came the fire truck, a herd of guys on motorcycles, and 4H kids with goats. The thing about a parade in a town like Bear Lake is that most of the citizens are in the parade, which doesn't leave much of a crowd to watch it. We stood side by side through the whole thing and the whole time I felt bad, like I didn't deserve to be standing there with her, and she didn't deserve to be going on a date with me.

109

CHAPTER NINETEEN

Sunday Morning, Early

The guy on the floor with the exploded chest was still alive. He wasn't supposed to be, but he was. His head rolled limply to one side and his body sprawled bonelessly, but his mouth was still opening and closing as if I'd shot him in the middle of a statement he wanted to finish. A glob of blood slid out of his mouth and down his chin.

Why wasn't he dead? He was supposed to be dead! He had a great big raggedy hole in his chest that was oozing blood. There was something pulsing behind the blood, and I didn't think it was his heart. He grinned at me nastily and hissed, "I'm gonna kill your friends for this. I'll get that fairy bitch and that eunuch that lives with you all and the dogs too."

Oh, Jesus, how does he know about fairies? How did he find out where I live? He rolled onto his hands and knees and, using the wall to steady himself, began a slow painful climb to his feet.

I recoiled and blundered backwards against the wall, and all kinds of stuff fell onto the floor: the pictures of my mom and dad, my hat and coat, some of Sally's metal cut outs. He slapped one blood-stained hand on the wall, making a hand print, and laughed. Then he did it again and again like a horrible parody of Bryan.

The air was as thick as water. I couldn't organize my hands and feet. I couldn't get off the ground to fly. He pushed himself away from the wall and staggered toward me, waving his bloody hands. I scrabbled sideways along the wall, fighting the thick viscous air. His mouth twisted in a ferocious grin. "I'm coming for you, I'm coming for you-oo-oo," he sang. "I'm coming, hee hee hee."

I struggled to fly but the air was nearly solid, and I was trapped like a fly in jam. Desperately, I tried to switch to fairy time, but it didn't work. I tried again and again but could not make the change.

My back hit the closed door. The militia guy held out one hand, pointed a finger at me like a pistol and whispered, "Bang."

It was a curse. I couldn't understand how a normal human could have the power to do a curse, but he had the power, and the curse sank into my chest like a poisoned bullet. I could feel it disintegrating in my stomach. I could actually feel shooting pains as it sank into my GI track.

I held out my hands, maybe to plead with him or maybe to fight him off, and smears of blood ran up my arms, across my chest and curled around my neck and into my hair. The blood imprinted itself in me in sinuous vine patterns like Maori art.

Someone was screaming and the sound filled the cabin, reverberating in the hot yellow of the lamp light.

Poochie erupted from the bed, barking hysterically, and I woke up all twisted in the blankets, covered in sweat, with my heart trying to punch its way out of my chest. I clutched the blanket to myself like a little kid and just tried to breath until I'd sort of calmed down.

"Hey, Poochie. It was just a nightmare," I whispered. But I took a quick look around to make sure it had just been a bad dream. My pictures were still on the wall, and my hat and coat were still on the hooks by the door. Sally's metal animal cutouts dangled from nails.

Poochie approached me cautiously and sniffed my fingers. "It's okay," I told him, even though I didn't feel okay at all. He gave me a dirty look, yawned to let me know that I had disturbed his sleep, and curled up in the tangled blanket. He was ready to go back to bed.

But I was wide-awake and my heart was spinning in my chest like a fan blade. Poochie didn't know that I'd killed someone. Sally didn't know either. And Taylor didn't know.

Taylor. Christ, I was going to be hosting a visit that day. A first date, almost. I was supposed to show her and her kid a good time.

Jesus, I wasn't in the mood. I wanted to curl back up in bed and never get out again. I didn't feel like myself. I felt . . . scared. Like the dead militia guy was out there in fairy time rampaging around, trying to get back to real time so he could come to Secret Lake and get his revenge on us like the undead in a horror movie. I could feel him hovering just out of sight. It didn't do any good to tell myself that he was dead.

I got up and staggered into the bathroom. Maybe because my insides felt dirty, I needed to clean the outside of myself. I took a shower, washed my hair, shaved. I dug down deep into my chest of drawers and resurrected an old t-shirt—the only clean one I had—which I never wear because it's too big. It was blue with the slogan "I Am the Lord of the Dance" printed on it in hot pink: Sally's design for an equinox dance years ago.

I dragged myself down to Sally's cabin and found her sitting on a porch drinking her shade coffee. That's another system broken: Coffee plantations have replaced shade with sun so the migrating birds have no winter home. I dropped into a chair. I didn't look at Sally.

She said, "I miss the birds."

I said, "I killed someone yesterday."

She set her coffee cup down carefully and turned toward me. Her eyes searched my face. "Who?"

"A militia guy."

"Are we in trouble?"

"No. No one will know because I did it in fairy time. He's just disappeared. Along with the militia's cash." That reminded me: I needed to bash open that metal box to find out what was in it. I hoped more cash.

She said, "So that's alright then." But she was watching my face, so she added, "Isn't it?"

"No. Well, yes, if you mean are we safe. We are."

But I could've left him alive. I could've just stranded him in fairy time. I didn't have to kill him. But, at the time, I hadn't felt like just stomping into the office and exiling him. I'd wanted to kill him.

Sally looked a bit impatient. She's a raven and ravens eat dead bodies. They kill, too. "Why are you feeling bad about this? Killing one of those militia assholes? I'd say score one for our team."

But that was the problem, wasn't it? Score one for our team? I killed him because I wanted to because I was angry. I hadn't been thinking of myself as part of a cycle of life that included the militia guy, a man that someone probably loved. I'd just acted from rage.

I didn't try to explain to Sally. I just let out a long sigh and changed the subject.

"I invited a friend and her kid to come out this afternoon."

Sally looked wary. "Who? Does this friend know about

us?" She meant know about fairies the way Arne and Charlie knew.

"She doesn't know. She's just a nice person who has a weird kid. She says he likes swimming."

We let a long silence stretch out, both of us staring at nothing. My mother had tried to keep me from growing up to be my dad. I remembered my dream about a picnic with Taylor: no comfort. I didn't want to comfort myself over acting like a wolf. I didn't want to make excuses, rationalize it. I didn't think I had the right to do that.

But I knew I was going to live with it. We have to cut the big bad things down to a size we can live with. That's something fairies and humans have in common.

So I got up. I needed something to do to fill the time before Taylor and Bryan showed up. Time to go bash in a metal box.

CHAPTER TWENTY:

Still Sunday

The box did contain cash, lots and lots of it in big bills. I'd have no trouble getting Arne out. Funny how that did not thrill me to pieces.

Probably the militia would think their guy just took their money and ran, though they'd be puzzled about why he didn't leave in his truck. I thought about that, about how his friends would think he'd robbed and betrayed them. They'd think he was, in their terms, a bad person. I felt kind of bad about that because death is final. In my terms he *was* a bad person but, now that he was dead, he would never get a chance to be good in anyone's eyes.

Which led me to thinking about the Congressman, the Russians and the trappers: also bad people in my eyes. What were they doing? Sitting around chatting and drinking coffee forever, I suppose. The world could go to hell around them, and they wouldn't even know. Wars for resources, mass extinctions, the deaths of millions from starvation, the deaths of people right here because the fucking Congressman thought people should just make their own happiness and didn't need government—blah, blah, blah.

The irony was that I probably hadn't harmed them. Heck, here there could be a nuclear war, and over there in fairy time they'd still be sitting around in the woods drinking coffee and chatting.

I thought maybe I'd go visit them every now and then.

I heard the crunch of wheels on the road: Taylor and Bryan. I got out on my porch and hailed them, and Taylor pulled her car in next to my cabin. It took a few minutes for her to extract herself; she had a ton of kid maintenance stuff along. I scooped a bag of clothes out of her arms. "Moving in?" I asked, then realized that my joke had embarrassed her. "Come on up on the porch and we'll unload some of this."

She got Bryan by one arm to stop him from spinning. Then she inhaled a lungful of pine-scented air and gazed around at our forest and lake. "Hey, thanks for inviting us out. This is a real treat." She meant it too. "It's all so lovely and peaceful." She turned to me, "I envy you living here."

I tried to smile back but was having trouble meeting her eyes. I felt like a fake, pretending to be a nice guy, hosting this little jaunt while carrying around a black hole in my conscience. "Yes. It is peaceful."

After we dumped her stuff in the cabin, I took them down to the dock and showed them the canoe. Bryan was vibrating and hissing. Taylor held his hand to keep him from jumping into the water.

"So . . ." I asked, "can he go canoeing? Would he like that?"

"I think he would. We can try it." I held the life jackets out, and Taylor strapped herself in. She manhandled Bryan into his, working around the constant jumping.

I loaded Taylor in first and she sat down. Then she held up her arms and wheedled Bryan into jumping into the canoe. I thought for a moment that they'd both end up swimming, but they managed to keep the canoe right side up. I grinned, "I should have told you the three rules about boating."

She smiled up at me. "Okay, what are the three rules about boating?"

"The boat goes in the water, you go in the boat, and the water stays out of the boat."

She nodded, pretending seriousness. "Aye, aye, Captain."

So I demonstrated by clambering in awkwardly, nearly tipping the canoe myself. The damn things seem to be designed to go sideways on you.

I handed her a paddle and we set out with Taylor eagerly surveying the lake and me at the back, steering. Bryan didn't know what to make of the experience. He tried to bounce, but found it difficult from his position on the bottom of the canoe. His hissing increased and morphed into repeated hoots. Then he discovered the joys of splashing one hand in the water, which made the canoe tilt. I decided to keep us near the shore.

We circumnavigated the lake, lingering at the mouth of the stream where dragonflies were dancing over the water plants. The aspen sisters were singing. I could hear the music, but Taylor couldn't. The singing comes from the flicker of their leaves in the breeze, olive green on one side and silvery green on the other.

Bryan stopped splashing when he noticed the water itself as something to look at rather than to feel. He leaned over the side of the canoe and stared, fascinated, into the golden and russet depths. Taylor and I leaned the other way to compensate and kept on paddling.

The sun was up, but the air over the water was still cool and gently breezy. A raven circled overhead and lit in a tree to caw, a sound that has always seemed lonely to me but often draws Sally out of the cabin to caw back. I could see her on the dock watching the raven and watching us, and I wondered if she would try to feed Taylor some cake. I decided to intervene if she did.

I thought about what it would be like if Taylor lived at the lake. She was turning out to be the kind of person who enjoys things quietly. In her way, she was as sensual as Bryan; I watched her turning her cheek in and out of the breeze while she allowed her hair to drift across her face. She, too, liked to trail her fingers in the water.

We paddled past the crying rock, but I didn't say anything to draw her attention to it. Instead I started talking about trees. "Do you know tree species?"

"Just the obvious ones."

"That one's a sugar maple. It's very, very old."

She nodded. "Its grand, isn't it? Like," she groped for a metaphor, "like an elephant? Big and clumsy but very majestic?"

I liked the comparison but didn't like thinking about the demise of the wild elephants. She shook her shoulders in enjoyment of the sun's heat across her back. I was enjoying the feeling, too, of bright cool air and hot sunshine on my skin.

By the time we got back to the dock, she'd nearly melted with relaxation. I realized that I'd gotten so used to Bryan that I hadn't noticed his change to "off" mode. He was nearly asleep.

"Look at Bryan," I said. She nodded and explained, "It's probably about four o'clock. You could almost tell time by him. He's six hours on, six off, regular."

Jeez, I thought, *how do you sleep?* But I didn't ask. Instead, we pulled up to the dock, tied up and clambered out, me first so Taylor could hoist Bryan up for me to lift. He didn't like being touched by anyone but Taylor and got a little cranky. She carried him from the dock up to Sally's front porch.

I hollered, "Hey, Sally!" to let her know we were coming, but Charlie answered the door. He stepped out to shake hands with Taylor, but quickly observed that she had her arms full. Sally appeared in the door behind him, her hair in a cloud of curls and a bit of apple stuck on her cheek.

We did the meet and greet thing, and both Sally and Charlie cooed over the sleepy child. At Sally's suggestion, we made a nest for him out of a crocheted throw on the couch. Bryan curled up like a baby fawn and zonked out.

"He's down for the count," Sally observed.

"His on button flipped to off," Taylor explained.

We all shuffled in a herd over to the table which Sally had already set with her hand-thrown ceramic dishes and yard sale placemats. She had a sprig of goldenrod in a glass as a centerpiece.

The cake, a marvel of blueberries, apples, and walnuts with a lovely brown sugar crumble crust, sat in a place of honor in the middle of the table. I tried to catch Sally's eye, but she wasn't going to let that happen, so I waved Taylor into a seat and said, "Eat, drink with no obligation to you or yours."

Sally rolled her eyes and sighed. Sally got her lover that way, but I've never wanted a devotee. I've never even wanted a roommate.

Not until now. The thought was in my head. It came from how comfortable we all were chatting and eating in Sally's kitchen. Taylor seemed to actually like Sally's eccentric taste in décor. She admired the cross-stitch hand towels, grinned at the pink flamingo, and expressed a liking for the yellow paint on the walls.

"Brightens the place up in the winter," said Sally, as she poured ice tea from her silver pitcher into her set of glasses decorated with palm trees and party hats.

We munched our way through the cake, sipped coffee afterwards and generally lolled about decadently. I realized that my mood had lightened, and I wondered: *Is this how bad people do bad things—by forgiving themselves?* Or maybe really bad people just didn't care. I needed to do something to atone. I couldn't atone to the militia guy, but maybe I could atone some way to life itself.

Sally asked, "Hey, Bobby, why the somber look?" and suddenly they were all staring at me. I shook my head, trying not to look defensive. "Not somber: satiated. I could almost join Bryan on the couch."

Sally said, "What you need is to go for a walk."

The look of concern on Taylor's face lifted. "Would you like that?" she asked. "A short one?"

"I'll wash up." Charlie stood up and started collecting plates.

"Oh, I'll help," said Taylor, grabbing the empty cake pan.

"No, you let Bobby take you out on one of the paths."

So that's how we ended up sitting on the crying rock, looking at the water and leaning on each other's shoulders since the top of the rock is really not big enough for two. Taylor told me that she'd had a wonderful day and that she was grateful. That hurt some: her being grateful to me. I realized that I was grateful to the two of them for coming out. Really grateful. They were, to me, like a bandage on a wound.

CHAPTER TWENTY-ONE:

Monday

I showed up at the jail bright and early Monday morning with a bag of money and an attitude. The little old lady, the one I glamoured into thinking she had cervical cancer, was behind the desk. She cringed back in her seat as I approached which made me feel good in a bad kind of way.

"I'm here to get Mr. Svenson," I told her. "What's the bill?" She turned to her computer, punched a bunch of keys, and printed out a total. Remember how she's said before that she couldn't tell me the cost? Now all of a sudden she could. In fact, she couldn't give me the cost fast enough.

I counted out the bills one at a time, making a big ceremony of it. Then I leaned over the counter and said, glamouring like crazy, "The doctor is wrong. You do have cancer. You'd better do something about that, or you will die."

She had one of those rolling chairs, and she gave her desk a shove and rolled back until she hit a file cabinet.

I grinned at her cheerfully. "Now get me Arne Svenson." She stabbed an intercom button and babbled, without taking her eyes off me, "John? It's Shelley. Get Mr. Svenson, please? He needs to be checked out."

John said something back, and she pointed to a chair on the far side of the room. "You can wait over there, sir."

So I rated a "sir" now, huh? It shouldn't pay to be mean to people, but sometimes it does. I slouched across the room to a chair and sat down to wait.

They took frickin' forever. An hour and ten minutes. I got really well-acquainted with their waiting room. Plastic chairs. Beige walls. A thick, solid door that led back to the off-limits area. Ugly plastic flowers coated with dust.

No one came in. I heard the occasional shout, usually followed by laughter. I got increasingly pissed off.

But finally the door opened and a militia guy stepped through, followed by Arne. I stood up and called, "Hey, buddy." The sight of him didn't make me feel relieved or triumphant or even a little bit happy.

Instead I felt shocked: Arne had shrunk. He looked tiny and fragile, a bent-over little old man who shuffled along with his hands clasped on the front of his jeans as if afraid his pants were going to fall down.

I must've moaned or gasped or something because he looked up, tried to smile, and said, "Took you long enough, asshole." Then, "Where's Poochie?"

CHAPTER TWENTY-TWO:

A Month Later

My mother told stories. She told them from when I was born right up to her death. Some of the stories were traditional from the Ojibwa people, others traditional from hare clan fairies, and some came from her imagination. This story she made up just for me:

Wild Hare was hopping around our forest up the hill where the stream starts, and he smelled Wolf. He could hear Wolf, too, mumbling to himself. Wolf was saying, "Little Hare, Little Hare, I can smell you."

Wild Hare crouched behind a tree stump and merged himself right into the wood. But he knew the stump wouldn't protect him. He knew he'd be seen when Wolf got closer. Wolf's voice was already closing in, and Wild Hare could smell his hot breath and hear the crunch of his big paws in the dry leaves of the forest.

So Wild Hare decided to use his avoidance skills as best he could. He shot out of his hiding place and ran in a zigzag down the hill. He made his hops small and close together so as to leave a trail, but when he got to the stream, he made a huge leap sideways, a good ten feet. He wanted Wolf to think he'd crossed the stream. He made three more big hops, then one across the stream and one back, hops that were so huge they were almost like flying. Then he flung himself behind a tree and peeked out to see what Wolf was doing.

Wolf was sniffing along the far edge of the stream, looking for Wild Hare's trail. He had his back toward Wild Hare, so Hare took off uphill. He tried to fly, but the ground dragged on his tired feet and his body felt heavy. He tried to go to fairy time but couldn't concentrate, couldn't make it work. Wild Hare scrambled and jumped and hopped in panic, but knew he wasn't moving fast enough. He scurried behind an old tree, and there he got an idea.

The tree was an ancient birch, mossy and soft with rot. It tilted like a drunk about to fall over. Wild Hare crouched behind the tree and waited for Wolf.

Wolf was laughing and singing as he climbed up the hillside, "Little Hare, Little Hare, all your rabbit tricks can't save you. This is the day I get to eat."

Wild Hare peeked around the tree. Timing was everything. He was almost sick with fear—but angry, too, and determined. Wild Hare held off until Wolf was just downhill from the tree. Then he flung all of his meager weight against the rotten trunk of the aged birch, hit it as hard as he could.

The tree teetered on its old frail roots, then—heavily, mightily, and with a tremendous ground-shaking crash—it fell over. The bottom of the trunk caught Wild Hare and sent him flying in a crazy arc through the air. Then a branch whacked him and slammed him into the ground. Wild Hare was smashed against the forest floor, unable to move. He wriggled and squirmed, fueled by rage and frustration, but could not escape the weight of the branch.

"Oh, Little Hare," the wolf sighed. "You shouldn't have tried to kill me. You killed yourself instead!"

And that's how the trickster tricked himself.

CHAPTER TWENTY-THREE:

Another Monday

"Do you believe in God," she asked.

"No."

"I don't either."

I snorted with surprise. "Then why ask about it?"

"Oh, just wondering. It's so peaceful here." She tilted her face back and smiled into the sun. "I guess the peacefulness makes me philosophical."

Taylor and I were courting, an unfamiliar ritual for me. Usually I just move in with the glamour, have fun for as long as it lasts, and move on. But I didn't want to treat Taylor that way. I wanted her to like me even though I didn't deserve to be liked. I knew at some point I was going to have to tell her about killing the militia guy. I'd have to tell her about fairies, too, but that was different. She'd probably like that once she believed it.

Our usual date was to meet out at the lake. Sometimes we went canoeing, which Bryan loved, and sometimes we just sat out on the porch with some dinner and some wine after Bryan went into "off" mode. We took Bryan for walks—which meant keeping him from putting things in his mouth—but also included Taylor listening to me being a bore about trees, plants, and nutrition cycles.

And we talked. We talked about all sorts of things: Bryan, her job, her previous marriage to an alcoholic abuser. Her family of religious nuts. Her putting herself through college to study literature, and her burden with student debt. Turns out I can be a good listener because I really didn't talk about myself much. I mostly listened.

It was strange to be with a woman and not ever glamour her. I did glamour Bryan every now and then. Poor Taylor thought I was really good with children. She said it was so sweet the way Bryan calmed down in my presence.

I thought: *I'll explain how that works someday.*

The day she asked about God, we were out on the crying rock. It was an afternoon so lovely and pine-scented under a hard blue sky that it was almost possible to be happy. Bryan was on "off" mode—because he was tired—up at the cabin under Charlie's watchful eye. Sally was almost certainly watching us through binoculars. And that's when Taylor started talking about religion.

I told her, "I don't believe in God, and I really hate people."

She laughed, startled. "Including me?"

"No, I'll make an exception for you. But people in general—my friend Mrs. Allen says that mankind was created in the image of God, but I think people made God in their own image and worship themselves. And that's why they're destroying everything."

I'm a barrel of fun on a beautiful day. Well, she needed to find out what I was really like before we got in too deep.

Taylor tilted her head back and gazed at the sky. "I don't know. I feel like life doesn't come with an instruction manual. Or there are too many different ones competing with each other. We're all just muddling along."

I mulled that over. But the sight of the aspen sisters singing in the breeze made me object. "Humans were given this wonderful world. They were given the cycles. They had a fucking instruction manual right there in front of their eyes, and they still fucked everything up."

She looked around thoughtfully. "I guess most people don't see nature that way. I mean as an instruction manual about what to value."

"I guess not." My voice was loaded with bitterness.

She gave me a quick side glance and said, "I know that everything is getting ruined. I'm afraid of climate change; I have a child to raise." She paused, thinking. "I just can't live with all that anger. I just can't. I try to do my best and not be part of the problem. That's the only thing I can think of to do: love my child and not make everything worse."

She looked like she might start crying, but she gave her face a quick wipe with her sleeve and laughed. "That's as far as I go with a religion! I know that everything is going down the drain. People have done horrible things and made horrible suffering for the world before. I need to be able to look back on my life and know that I did my best."

She shrugged, a little embarrassed, I guess. But I thought of my mother and how much she would've liked Taylor. And I thought of the Wild Hare and Wolf story my mother told me when I was a kid. And I thought about what Taylor meant by doing her best.

A stiff breeze prickled my skin and Taylor shivered. I wrapped my arms around her shoulder and pulled her tight against my chest, and she nestled her face against my neck. We sat like that for a long time while the night settled gently around us.

CHAPTER TWENTY-FOUR:

Sunday Morning

I pulled into Mrs. Allen's driveway and realized that I'd never been inside her house. I don't know why that thought came into my head; I haven't been in most people's houses. I think it was a measure of how curious I'd gotten about her. I wondered if she had fake flowers in bowls distributed around her living room because she sure had enough of them around her porch.

Her potted plants had succumbed to the chilly nights and had been replaced with plastic roses in pink and white. Fall had set in, and the constant prickle of smoke in the air had been replaced by a biting cold in the mornings and a tangy pine-scented freshness in the afternoons. The sky was a hard smooth blue that almost looked solid, and the stars had returned to the nighttime sky. It was almost possible to forget how bad everything had gotten, almost possible to imagine a future. Almost.

I watched her negotiate her front steps. She held onto the porch rail for balance and tottered. *She's finally beginning to act old,* I thought. One of these days she wasn't going to go to church anymore. I jumped out of the car and grabbed her elbow. To my surprise, she leaned on me.

"Good morning, Mr. Fallon. I can't seem to quite get my sea legs today."

"Maybe it's the cold," I suggested. I opened the car door. She sank onto the seat.

"I don't think so," she said. Then she gathered her huge purse into her lap and pulled her legs and feet into the car. I closed the door gently and got in the driver's side. I was kind of slow getting the car started. I was thinking about how routines can be taken for granted until they are suddenly broken. I didn't know if our routine was important to Mrs. Allen except as transportation and didn't have any way to ask, but the Sunday drives with Mrs. Allen had become important to me. I let my breath out in a long sigh, threw the car into reverse, and backed out of the driveway.

A little cluster of kids on the corner stared at us as we passed, mouths tightly closed, expressionless. Most of the trailers had their windows blocked with bed sheets or cardboard, as blank as closed eyes. I imagined the kids as sentries or lookouts. Their heads turned as we passed, tracking us.

I said, "Those kids give me the creeps."

Mrs. Allen said, "Everyone is hiding something these days, seems like."

Was that meant for me? No, I was just being paranoid. No one had connected the disappearance of the Congressman or the death of the militia guy with me. There was a huge amount of uproar, of course. But no connection.

My mind had been going over and over the death of the militia man constantly for weeks, as if by thinking I was performing some kind of protective magic. Or building a wall—a wall to keep others out and myself within. I realized that I had driven all the way out to the highway without responding to her comment.

"Yeah," I said. "Seems that way to me too."

"No one trusts anyone else."

It occurred to me that *she* was fishing this time. She was feeling me out, just as I had done so many times to her. I reminded myself that she couldn't possibly be trying to connect me to my crimes. Maybe she was probing to see if she could share something about herself? I didn't feel any excitement about that; in fact, I almost didn't want to know her secrets anymore. I didn't think I deserved to know. So I just said, "Sometimes people have secrets they can't share because..." and my voice dried up. I didn't know how to finish the sentence.

"Reputation?" she suggested.

"Yeah, or consequences."

We stewed in our separate thoughts for awhile, and then she did that mind-reading thing she does that makes me wonder if she has a little fairy in her somewhere. "When you fight a violent and mean enemy, it's difficult not to become violent and mean yourself."

See? Nail meet head. My hands jerked on the steering wheel. I kept my eyes straight ahead.

"It's hard to find a way to fight back that doesn't just lead to self-degradation." *She still talks like a school teacher*, I thought. But self-degradation was what I'd done, even if it was a ten-dollar word when just plain ol' shame was close enough.

"And it's important not to be too forgiving of one's sins, because that's how the sins become a pattern." She smiled but looked sad. "I'm a practicing Christian—emphasis on practicing! So I can get preachy at times."

"Well, I can't imagine you sinning much," I forced a teasing tone.

"Oh, I sin. I have sinned." I took a quick look at her. She was gazing out the window. "The sin of pride in my own righteousness. The sin of anger and hatred toward those

who do what I believe is wrong. I'm just thinking about that
. . . since we're on the way to church. And, to be honest,
one of my sins is contempt for the preacher." She turned
toward me, but her expression was inward, thoughtful. "He
makes it all too easy. Last week he tried to convince us that
all we had to do was accept Jesus into our hearts and all
would be forgiven."

I had to laugh at that. "So why do you go?"

"I still believe in the teachings of Jesus, even if I don't
always live up to them. But I think that forgiveness for sin
must be based on actions. Different actions, without sin."

The "Report All Aliens" sign hove into view, and I saw her
lips tighten in a look of anger or disgust.

I wanted to ask her who else she hated, but that was
too direct. So I asked, "How are you supposed to feel
towards people who do you wrong? Isn't getting mad kind
of natural?"

"Bob . . . " She paused and I wondered why she was
calling me by my first name. She never did that, not even in
high school. Everyone was Miss or Mr. "Bob, I know you are
not a believer, but Jesus, who I try to use as a guide, taught
that we were to fight evil without anger and hate toward
the evildoer. Fight the act, end the acts, prevent the acts,
but not become hateful ourselves. And sometimes I just find
that very hard."

Then she patted me on the shoulder. "Thank you for
listening to a sad old woman. You are a very patient young
man."

No, I was the guy who killed someone. But I didn't say
that.

CHAPTER TWENTY-SIX:

Sunday Night

He staggered up on the porch. I heard him and had just enough time to disentangle my feet from my blankets and swing my legs out of the bed before he appeared inside my room. I had no lights on but could see him clearly. His uniform was mussed and dirty with sticks and leaves, and his fuzz of hair was slick with sweat. His eyes were sunken into his swollen, pasty face like cinders in snow. But it was his chest that drew my attention; he had a hole the size of a medium pizza right where his heart used to be, gaping open and pulsing with thick, red blood.

"Why'd you do it?" I thought for one horrific moment that his voice was coming from the hole in his chest; the rhythmic opening and shutting looked like a huge mouth. I couldn't stop staring at it.

He stumbled closer and began to wave his arms. "Why'd you have to do it? Why me?"

I had a sudden fear that he would grab me with those waving arms and mash me up against that bloody hole in his chest. I'd be covered with his blood. I scrambled off the bed and out of his reach.

He clumsily re-oriented himself toward me and nearly lost his balance. I realized that he was blind; his arms waved randomly. The pulse in the hole seemed to be leading him, the blood reaching out, seeking me. I edged around him toward the door.

His sightless eyes tracked me and again he cried, "Why me? Why'd you do it? Why'd you kill me?"

I backed up until I hit the wall. I had to duck to dodge his swinging arms.

"I don't know!" I yelled. But I did know, and his flapping mouth with the loose red lips and the sightless eyes demanded an answer. "I did it for Danni. Because you guys killed Danni."

"I don't know nobody named Danni." He dropped his arms as if my answer had calmed him. "Why'd you do it when I don't know this Danni?" His shoulders slumped, defeated. He whined, "Why?"

I thought I heard running feet outside. Sally? Was Sally coming? I didn't want her to see this guy. "Come on," I told him, "Let's go outside." I felt around behind me, grabbed the doorknob, and swung the door open. "Let's go out on the porch together."

But he wasn't stupid. He knew I was just trying to get rid of him. The hole sucked up great gulps of pain out of the air and flapped out a thin, shrill whine, "Why'd you do it, why'd you do it, why'd you do it?"

"Because I was mad!" I screamed. I jolted up out of the dream, panting, sweating, terrified.

CHAPTER TWENTY-SEVEN:

Monday Morning

I got a call from Arne; he needed a ride into town to get some parts for his truck, which wasn't running again. I picked him up and drove him to the hardware store.

The hardware store functions like the cerebral cortex of Bear Lake; information is processed there. And, humans being not quite as bright as they claim to be, the information processing often takes the form of gossip, speculation, exaggeration, and just plain making shit up. That day, when Arne and I walked into the store, it was plain that we'd interrupted a conversation in progress. And a paranoid one, too, given how six pairs of eyes swiveled in our direction and all talk ceased.

Arne stopped so abruptly that I almost bumped into him. "What?" he asked.

Then the sales guy, the stocky young man, recognized Arne as a frequent customer and hailed him with friendliness. The group opened up to admit us and suddenly everyone was trying to catch us up on the latest.

"Three people from right here in Bear Lake were arrested for terrorism!"

"Who would've thought an old lady schoolteacher . . . "

"She was my teacher when I was in high school, and I always suspected her of being a liberal."

"What?" I interrupted. "What're you all talking about?"

Sales Guy said, "Haven't you heard? Old Mrs. Allen and the Moores that run the motel were running some kind of underground railroad for terrorists. They were caught with a Muslim woman who's wanted for some crime against the state."

I felt like I'd been hit in the stomach with an ax.

"That can't be right," I stuttered. "She's a Christian. Goes to church every Sunday. I drive her." And I thought: *That explains going to a church she doesn't believe in— cover.*

"Well, she was part of it," Sales Guy assured me. I checked the faces of the group: all guys, all gleeful at the drama but trying to look solemn and serious like this wasn't the most exciting thing that had happened since the Congressman disappeared.

And right on cue one of them spoke up, "I bet this has something to do with Congressman Van Dusan disappearing! I bet they killed him!"

"That militia guy who stole the money has to have something to do with this too!" added someone. "You know he stole the militia money, right? He must've been a traitor."

"That was Jack Munson, right? I knew him in high school. He was an asshole." Nearly everyone in Bear Lake went to high school with everyone else.

"They had to all be in it together!" The group was halfway to solving the big, bad conspiracy. I whispered to Arne, "I got things to do." He tore his eyes and ears from the fascinating conversation. "Oh, yeah, hey, I need some spark plugs," he asked the sales guy.

"Huh?" I watched the jolt as Sales Guy remembered he was supposed to be working. "Oh, spark plugs. Follow me.

I'll be right back," he called to the talkers.

We didn't have any trouble walking out without paying, even though by the time we got done, Arne was lugging a big box of car stuff and I had some too. I told Arne to go wild because I knew we'd never be more than a mild distraction. Not with everyone's high school teacher in jail.

"Wow, our very own radical underground terrorist cell, and it's Mrs. Allen and the Moores. Who'da thunk it?" Arne kept shaking his head in amazement.

"Assholes, that's who believes it. Assholes." I threw my bag of clanking metallic stuff into the back seat and flung myself behind the driver's wheel. Arne got in more circumspectly and gave me a cautious look.

"I didn't know you liked ol' Mrs A. I thought you were kind of scared of her like everyone else."

"I'm still scared of her." I jammed the car into gear and did a u-turn. It's legal. I headed south toward our house.

Arne said, "Hey, aren't we going to pick up some groceries too? I thought we were going to the store."

I loosened my death grip on the steering wheel. I needed a chance to think. "Are you and Poochie going to starve?" I asked.

"Well, no, not if I can eat at Sally's tomorrow."

"Then we'll grocery shop later." We were driving by the gun shop. If the hardware store was the cerebral cortex of Bear Lake, the gun shop was the amygdala, and fear and mindless belligerence were out in force that morning. The place bristled with guys in black with big, complicated guns, the kind designed for warfare. There must have been ten of them staked out all along the road and glaring into the bright fall air, just itching for a brigade of terrorists to come marching up the highway.

Some of those guys were real vets with real military experience but most were wannabes. They'd run if a real army showed up. I wasn't a real army. How the hell was I going to break three old people out of jail? And a Muslim woman too.

I was concentrating on that so much that I almost didn't hear Arne until he leaned toward me and asked, "Hey, Bobby what's eating you?"

"Huh? Nothing, I mean something—those folks in jail. That's eating me."

He just stared at me. Arne had actually benefited by time in jail; he'd dried out. His eyes looked brighter, more focused and he was a little cleaner. I could almost see the squirrel on the treadmill in his head. Finally he spoke, "I don't think you can do much about that. She'll get a lawyer. She's a smart lady."

Well, he was right about that. She was a smart lady. But I still had to get her out.

the Equinox

I settled with my back up against an aged balsam fir and waited for the festivities to start. I felt about as festive as roadkill. There was an air of defiance to Sally's party. Usually equinox dances sort of organize themselves: lots of talk and sometimes arguments about who wanted to host and where, but gradually the details always got worked out, and folks showed up and the parties always took off in the end. But we didn't have a big crowd that equinox and weren't going to get one.

Sally and Charlie had hung Christmas lights in the trees, Sally by flying and Charlie up on a ladder. The lights were run off a power cord from the last cabin in the row. Not traditional, but that's what happens when a raven plans things. We weren't going to have a bonfire either, so she'd made a weird centerpiece for the dance out of found objects. Well, she made the rest of us find objects. Everyone had to bring something "meaningful" as the price of admission. The meaningful objects were piled up on one of her quilts in a little clearing, which was actually an overgrown piece of parking lot from back when the resort had summer crowds.

I thought: *This resort is one of the few places on earth were the human crowds are less, not more. I'll drink to that!* And I had a slug of beer.

Sam and Ronnie and Betty and their mob of water fairies straggled in from the spring—the gals with dried flowers in their hair—looking like hippies. The kids ran amok, except they were flying, not running. Air tag . . . or just burning off energy. The found objects were rocks carried down the trail from the spring. To make the colors show, they'd poured water over the rocks, which soaked the quilt and the other objects. Sally was thrilled. There was lots of laughing and chatter.

I checked the sky: early evening.

Arne drove up a little later. He jumped down from his newly-drivable truck, Poochie at his heels. Sally waved him over and everyone said hi, and I heard commiserations about his incarceration and so on. He gave me a wave and headed into Sally's cabin. A moment later he was backed up to my tree with a beer of his own.

"So . . . this is it?" Arne knew about fairy dances, but he'd never been invited to one before.

"Not sure," I said. "There might be some more later." As I spoke an old van grumbled its way up the drive and halted by my cabin. I watched a bunch of coyotes and coyote mixes climb out: three men, two women, some teenagers, a coupla' kids, and a dog that looked like a coyote mix too. They were all lean and lanky with that sharp, wary look. The women had lots and lots of grayish brown hair and wore colorful dresses that swirled around their ankles. They had provisions in baskets, and the alpha woman carried a deer antler. Sally came down out of a tree to greet them.

The oldest one held out a basket of blueberries and said, "Greetings. Eat and drink with no obligation to you and yours." Sally accepted the basket and the deer antler. She asked, "And what is the meaning of your offering?"

"We heard that you were hares up here, so we thought you might like the berries. The basket is old. It's woven from grass. Supposed to be Objibwa." She didn't have to explain the antler.

"Well, thanks." Sally was impressed. "Come on up and meet everyone."

Real fairies usually aren't huggers or hand shakers, partly because they don't spend a lot of time around people and don't value human ways, but also because what you see—the human-appearing form—is not real. It's their glamour maxing out, a movie project version of themselves. The projection is solid, don't get me wrong. It's just not the way they really are.

So our group of mixes and humans and fairies didn't shake hands or hug. We just all got in a raggedly circle and said our names and hello and glad to meetcha and eat, drink, with no obligations to you and yours, etc., and proceeded to do just that.

While we feasted, we got a couple more carloads of coyotes from down south—the coyotes have adapted to town life better than the rest of us—and some more hares from somewhere to the west of us. We even got a coupla' families of water fairies from the boundary lakes—well, they used to be from the boundary lakes, but the mining drove them off. Now they live up in Canada, but they came down for old time's sake. Everyone added food and beverages—mostly beer—to the party and joined in with the eating and drinking.

No, it wasn't a crowd like old times, but it was a pretty good turn out anyway. I've been to fairy dances that were so big we had to move to fairy time to keep from having the county out with noise complaints. But we got more than Sally was expecting, so she was happy.

Then we drank and yakked and told stories. I didn't tell the story about killing the militia guy, but the exiling of the Congressman was a great story. Everyone loved that he was still out in the woods, and some wanted me to fly them out to visit just to laugh at him, but I didn't want to leave the party. Everyone had a story to tell, and a lot of them were stories about fighting back, especially the coyotes.

After everyone was stuffed, the party went into post-food recovery mode. Kids fell asleep. Adults flopped on the ground, leaned against trees, or collapsed into the folding chairs that Sally had set out. Beers hissed open and bottles of hard liquor got slugged down, passing from mouth to mouth.

I went back to my tree and watched the crowd—I like to do that sometimes. Lots gathered in family groups, but some mixed it up, hares with coyotes. I watched a few younger couples sneak off into the woods. Not that sneaking was necessary—everyone knew what they were doing, and there were lots of grins and probably some reminiscences about other parties and other couplings.

I was comfortable just being with myself, so I was kind of surprised when an old coyote wandered over and asked if I wanted a little weed.

"Sure." I scooted to one side a bit to give him some leaning room on the tree. He settled down with an arthritic grunt and pulled out a blunt and a lighter from his coat pocket.

This guy looked half-starved like most coyotes do, and he was old, his face deeply grooved and bristly from a half-assed attempt at shaving. He had the high cheek bones and brownish skin that coyotes favor, and the power radiated out of him so strong I could see it as a faint glow.

I was real curious about him. "I'm Bob," I introduced

myself. "So where're you guys from?" His cheeks hollowed out as he inhaled. Then he tipped his head back, held the smoke for a few seconds, and let it out in a cloud.

"Al. Minneapolis." he said on the gasp of his exhale. "Got a big pack there." He nodded toward the group nearest the pile of found objects. "That's just some of us. We came up to get out of town for a while, get back to the trees."

I wondered what it was like to live in a city and decided that I didn't want to find out.

Skunkweed. I like that smell, even though it stinks if you aren't high yourself. He handed me the blunt, and I had a long inhale of my own. The top of my head lifted off.

"Nice place here," he said. I passed him the blunt, and he sank another lungful. "Thanks."

"That's really good weed," I told him.

"We grow it," he wheezed. Cough, cough. "Sell it too."

He had to be a really powerful fairy to live in the city selling weed and glamouring people all day long into seeing him as another human. Most pure fairies can't keep up the glamour for hours on end. I wondered how strong the rest of his crew was.

"So who all's with you?" I asked. "Family?"

"My sons and their wives. Over there." He pointed with the blunt. His sons were adults. Full fairy, but visible as a couple of guys with ponytails and leather jackets and boots. I thought: *I'll bet they're a motorcycle gang when they're back home in the Twin Cities.* And all of them powerful. Something to think about.

Sally interrupted us with a holler with regards to starting the dance. Darkness had fallen long ago—I hadn't noticed with all the chatter and food and booze. I climbed to my feet, and my head just kept on going until I was floating away like a lost balloon. Al grabbed me by one foot and yanked me back down. We stumbled toward the gathering, bumping shoulders like old buddies. I heard a scream of laughter from out in the woods, and someone in the crowd applauded loudly and yelled, "Go for it!" We were a tipsy bunch when we gathered around that pile of meaningful objects.

The gals and kids got things started. They held hands and rose up into the night sky in a spiraling circle, round and round and up and up. It didn't matter that they were dressed in everything from the coyote ladies' gowns to Sally's jeans. It didn't matter that they were all ages and sizes. No, that's wrong; it did matter, but in the right way. The dance was *supposed* to be a motley crew, supposed to be a bouquet of weeds and flowers.

The men began to chant. That's our part. We listened to each other and kind of felt for a rhythm. It started out tentative, just someone chuffing and someone whistling. Then, as more and more joined in, it got complicated and loud. Someone started hitting the off beats for some syncopation. Someone else started mixing up their clapping with stamping. I hummed until I got breathless, then started to snap my fingers and stomp my feet. Beside me Arne joined in with a raspy grunt. It occurred to me that Bryan would love this, and I had an impulse to twirl in place, but I didn't because I knew I'd lose my balance. I didn't want to fall on my ass, not yet anyway.

There's a point when the stomping and grunting and whistling and so on takes on a life of its own, and all the sounds merge into something bigger than the parts. It becomes alive, stronger than any individual. I stopped feeling like I might lose my balance. I felt like the intricate weaving of rhythm was holding me up. I began to bounce on my toes.

I tilted my head back to watch the women and kids. They were up far enough that I couldn't really see them any more—just black shapes against the soft, deep darkness of the night sky, silhouetted against the stars. Stars. It had been a summer without stars—too much smoke—but the recent rain had washed the smoke out the sky, and the galaxy was on display: countless lights of varying brightness, glowing threads of them, a flow across the sky. The women showed up as fluttering shapes against the silvery smear of the Milky Way. I saw Sally's mass of hair swing out from her shoulders and a coyote gal's long skirt whip around her legs.

It was our turn. I felt bad leaving Arne and Charlie on the ground because it feels so good to rise up into the sky for a dance. We spiraled upwards, but the other way around from the women, counter clockwise. We didn't hold hands, just swam through the air however the urge struck us. I rolled around and around until I was dizzy, and then I floated on my back with my arms out and gazed upwards.

The Milky Way was awesome in all its glory. I lay on the night air and stared up at the stars and something shifted so that I felt like I was looking down, as if the stars were spread out below me across the infinite darkness. As if I could fall and just keep falling forever.

I've heard different things about the universe: That it is ever-expanding, or that it is finite but it turns on itself so that if you could travel in one direction long enough you eventually come back to where you started. I've even heard that there are other universes out there—I guess inside some kind of vast space—beyond both my human and fairy abilities to understand. I can't comprehend the universe except to know it is much, much bigger than me.

I mean, there must be other life out there somewhere. Some other planet someplace that humans aren't fucking up. The vast, silent, slow cycles of the universe; the migrations of planets; the wheeling of galaxies; the life span of stars—whatever the shape and scope of the universe turns out to be—it's all beyond what humans can destroy.

I have always loved stars. But that night I loved them with a kind of desperation. I loved them because they would still be there—not each individual one because some would flame out as novas—but as a group, as a cycle, they would just keep on being stars long after my death.

I found some comfort in that.

CHAPTER TWENTY-NINE:

Two Days Later

I'd come up with a plan.

A fine misty rain was blessing Bear Lake. I leaned against the lone pine at the back edge of the parking lot behind the militia building. Two coyotes, John and Al, huddled with me—not because they cared about getting wet but because I cared. I wanted to pass them off as a couple of lawyers, and it wouldn't help if they were soaking wet.

Al took a last drag on his cigarette and tossed it onto the pavement. "We got this, Bobby," he told me.

I had my doubts. Dressed up in Charlie's suit and Arne's set of Sunday best, they looked more like a couple of down and out small town pool sharks than respectable lawyers. Neither set of clothes fit right, and besides, as full coyote fairies, both Al and John had that feral air that regular humans can sense even though they don't know what they are sensing.

I mean, they both looked reasonably human—they had the required eyes, ears, nose, legs, arms, and so on, but they still seemed hairy and boney somehow. Their demeanor was watchful, jeering, clever. Too many teeth were on display when they smiled.

Then again, maybe that clever, toothy look was appropriate for a coupla' lawyers.

"Okay," I said. "Hey, give me one?"

"Here." Al handed over the whole pack and the lighter. I shook a cig loose and took a couple of shots at lighting it, but my hands were shaking. Al and John grinned at me. John gave my arm a brief pat and said, "Hey, it's going to work. Your hare-brained idea, right?"

I grimaced. Then I thumbed the damn lighter and got the cig going. Took a deep drag and exhaled smoke like a dragon. They laughed.

"See ya." Al gave me a wave and the two took off across the parking lot, taking the umbrella with them. They were about halfway across when they vanished into real time. That left me standing under the tree in the fairy time rain. Who knew it rained in fairy time?

I sucked on the cigarette and shuffled back further under the tree. Everyone was going to get wet. Hopefully no one would die of hypothermia.

Jesus, I was nervous. I shifted from one foot to the other, walked in a tight circle, bounced up and down. I tried to stand still. Couldn't. I did more shifting and bouncing. Then it occurred to me that I could use the cig to tell time. How long did it take to smoke one? Maybe ten minutes? Ten minutes in fairy time was a lot more in real time. That meant they'd be back before I was done with one, if it all went right.

If it all went right. My mother said that stories made reality. She hadn't meant that literally, but I needed something to steady me, so I started narrating the tale as if my thoughts were controlling events:

Al and John walk around to the front of the militia building. They collapse their umbrella and go in. Psychobitch behind the counter, still worried about cancer even though she's been to the doc a dozen times, looks up and sees two slimy, weird guys in bad suits and immediately gets paranoid. They approach the counter and whip out some little squares of card stock with Sally's writing on it, and Al says, "We're legal representatives for Mrs. Allen, Mr. and Mrs. Moore, and the Muslim woman. We need to see them now."

And both glamour at her like a couple of semi trucks barreling down the road at a turtle on a crosswalk. Psychobitch doesn't stand a chance. At least in my story— the story I was telling myself—she didn't.

She just blinks, blinks, blinks and calls for an escort. They get a bored militia asshole who takes one look and thinks: "Terrorist-enabling scum going to fuck up our prosecution." But he leads them down to the visiting room anyway because it would fuck up a prosecution even more if the prisoners didn't get a lawyer. Or that used to matter anyway. I don't know if it still does. Back to the story. Al and John are glamouring at the militia guy full blast. Telling him to bring all of the prisoners, all at one time.

They wait in the dismal little visiting room until the militia guy shows up with everyone in handcuffs. As soon as Mrs. Allen sees the two coyotes, she objects. She says, "You aren't my lawyers." Because Mrs Allen for sure had a lawyer, and a good one, and of course she was going to try to run the show. But I'd foreseen this and the guys were prepared. Back to the story. They trot out the cover story, "We're aides to your lawyer."

They have to get the handcuffs off everyone, so they glamour at the militia guy: "Take off the cuffs for our conference time." Militia guy doesn't like that, but his mind is all fogged up, and he feels unsure of himself so he complies. Then he tells everyone to sit down. There aren't *enough chairs. The Moores get seated, but Mrs. Allen and the Muslim lady are still standing. The militia guy is getting pissed about that and uneasy and things are getting out of control.*

I wondered if things were really spiraling out of control in real life. I jumped back into the story and got things under control there.

Al says, "What are you afraid of—three senior citizens and that young lady? We know our legal rights." Militia guy is glaring like the glamour is maybe not working any more, so John, who's been standing near the militia guy on purpose, takes a step toward him and tasers the hell out of him. Militia guy falls on the floor, writhing and moaning.

Everyone starts babbling, and Al and John glamour them to all shut up.

Then Al starts frisking the militia guy. Since the militia guy is having a seizure on the floor, it takes a while to snag his keys. But once Al finds the keys, boom! Al and John shift everyone into fairy time.

Except militia guy of course. Al and John get the handcuffs off the prisoners and try to explain that they are escaping, but everyone is talking at once and scared. The coyotes get annoyed, yell at everyone to shut up. Then they herd everyone out of the building.

My cigarette was now down to nothing but the filter and ashes. What was taking them so long? Maybe I'd been smoking really fast. I felt dizzy. That was probably it: I'd been inhaling the damn thing like I could speed up time with each drag. I tried to shake the tension out of my back by dropping the butt on the ground and stomping on it.

I thought of everything that could go wrong. I imagined Al and John jumping the militia guy, grabbing for the gun, ladies screaming, more militia guys barging in . . .

And then suddenly there they were: stumbling, hunched over in the rain, a confused conga line of people in glaring orange jumpsuits and those stupid plastic sandals. It was a shock—I'd forgotten that everyone would be wearing jail clothes. I could hardly recognize Mrs. Allen without her pink sweater and her low-heeled pumps.

Al and John herded them my way, all of them asking questions and looking scared. But Mrs. Allen caught sight of me, and suddenly she was hurrying across the wet pavement in her wet flip flops, calling my name.

"Mr. Fallon! Are you here to help us?" Her hair was already in strings from the rain. She grabbed my hands. "Are these men friends of yours?'

"Yes, they are." I assured her. The conga line formed a circle around me. I took a quick look at the array of faces. Mr. Moore had his arm around Mrs. Moore's shoulders. They looked pathetic. She was trembling and seemed on the brink of hysteria, and he could hardly stand up. The Muslim gal was the calmest of the bunch. She had a pretty brown face with high cheekbones and almond eyes—maybe Asian of some kind? She wasn't wearing one of those scarves.

I asked her, "Do you speak English?"

"Yes." she snapped. Then she took a deep breath to steady herself. "Of course I do. I am a legal citizen, and I have papers to prove it. In the office." She waved her arm at the militia building. "They have my papers." She didn't have an accent. I felt sort of stupid for assuming that she'd be foreign.

Mr. Moore, shoulders hunched and face screwed up with worry, whispered, "Where is everyone? Shouldn't we be trying to hide?"

"What if they shoot us?" Mrs. Moore cried out. "What

if they shoot us for trying to escape? We need to run and hide!" That started everyone jabbering and yanking on my arm and waving their hands in the air.

I could see that I had to get control. "Stop talking everyone! Listen up," I barked at them. "There are no people around. No one is here but us. You're safe."

They didn't believe that, so they all kept right on talking and crying and yelling.

"Glamour them," I said to Al and John.

The two coyotes spoke in unison, "Be calm, people, and be quiet."

Everyone shut up, except Mrs. Moore who whimpered. They stared at the coyotes as if mesmerized.

"Be calm and listen to Bob," Al told them. "You are safe now. There is no one around to hurt you." Then he tore off his tie, shoved it in a wad in his shirt pocket, and starting slapping all of his other pockets for his cigarettes. I had his pack, so I handed it over. Everyone stared, fascinated, while he got one lit.

I wished I could glamour that well.

"Alright," I told the group of escapees. "Look around. Do you see anyone?"

There was no one in sight. No cars passing, no random pedestrians, no militia. The huddled group gazed around in confusion.

"Where is everyone?" the Muslim gal demanded. "Why aren't the cops out here?"

"We took care of that," I told her. "Like Al said, you are all safe now." They were not convinced. I had to give them something more. "I am going to explain something that you will have trouble believing." I made my tone as assured as I could, like I was Mrs. Allen giving a lesson to a class. "How many of you believe in God?" I scanned the circle of wet faces. "Mrs. Allen?"

"Yes," she said

"Mr. and Mrs. Moore?"

"We're Lutherans," he answered

"And you?" I asked since I didn't know her name. "Do you believe in Allah?"

"Well, I'm mostly secular, but a belief in Allah is fundamental to Islam," she informed me. That brought me up short. I didn't know how to process that, so I just kept going.

"So if you all believe in God, then you believe in the supernatural, right? Because God is a god, right? Supernatural?"

I got some baffled, reluctant nods. They were still looking around fearfully.

"So if you can believe in a god, then you can believe in other supernatural things too, right?"

"Angels!" whispered Mrs. Moore breathlessly. "Are you angels?" She was ready to fall to her knees, I swear, and I couldn't think of anyone who looked less like angels than the three of us. Al snorted rudely.

"Spirits," I corrected her. "These two are nature spirits from the prairie, and I am half nature spirit from the forest. We are spirits."

They all just stared at me.

"Look," I said to Al and John. "You guys need to leave, right? So why don't you just go, and when you vanish these guys will believe us about you being spirits because they'll see you disappear."

Al pointed at Mrs. Allen with his cigarette. "We are spirits. You'll see. Bob," he added, "I'll tell Sally and them that you're all okay."

"Sure, thanks." I meant it.

"And you all," Al told the group, glamouring like crazy, "Stop fooling around and hit the road. Bob can't hang out with you forever."

"Are you leaving?" Mrs. Allen asked. "Where are you going?"

"The guys are going home." I told her.

Mrs. Allen grabbed Al's hands to thank him but he slid away. "You folks just do what Bobby tells you, and maybe we'll see you in a couple of months," he told her.

"What do you mean a couple . . ." She didn't finish her question because they'd vanished. Everyone stared open-mouthed at the air once occupied by Al and John.

"My God," Mr. Moore whispered in awe. "Did you see that? They really were spirits."

"Yeah, coyote spirits." I said. "Remember that next time someone tells you that coyotes are vermin."

"Oh, I will." He was fervent and wide-eyed. They were all awe-struck. But I was wet, tired, and impatient. At the rate we were moving, it would be a couple of months' real time before I got back home.

"That's why there aren't any people here? Except us? You used a magic spell?" Mrs. Moore again, now even more likely to fall to her knees.

"Well, sort of. Anyway we're safe," I told her. They looked better. Stunned, uncomprehending, but no longer on the brink of hysteria. "Hey," I said, "we have to get out of the rain. Right? I have a ride lined up for you all, so let's get moving."

CHAPTER THIRTY:

Five Days Later

The plan was for Arne to pick us up at the "Report Aliens" sign. We had to walk across the empty town, the ladies stumbling in their flip flops. I soon realized it isn't possible to make old ladies hurry. I was conscious the whole way that the longer we took, the more real time would pass, but I couldn't get them moving faster than a shuffle. Once we got to the sign, I took us back into real time.

My little group of refugees nearly froze—we'd left fairy time wet and arrived back in regular time in the cold of late evening. I phoned Arne and told him to get his ass out to pick us up and grab some blankets or our rescued folks would be free but dead from hypothermia. While we waited, we hid from the eyes of passing traffic by huddling in the woods.

When Arne pulled up in his truck, we bundled the ladies into the cab, with Mrs. Allen and Mrs. Morris piled on top of each other and the Muslim gal jammed behind the seat on top of a bunch of tools. I crawled under a blanket in the back with Mr. Moore. Arne drove us to our resort, where we thawed everyone out with hot showers, tea, and soup. Then we stashed them in fairy time to rest and calm down.

While our refugees were relaxing, Sally caught me up on

what she knew of the local news, but she had no details. She and Charlie and Arne had stayed out of town as much as possible while I was gone, so all they'd heard was the lady Muslim terrorist had escaped, and one of the militia guys had been fired.

"Hey, I'm back."

"That's great! Welcome home!" Taylor sounded genuinely glad to hear from me, which kind of made me feel ashamed. It still seemed weird to me that I felt like I'd only been gone for an afternoon—a long afternoon—but to everyone else I was the guy they hadn't seen in five days.

"So," she said, "how was your trip?" I'd told her that I was going to help out some relatives and would be gone for a few days, but I didn't want to continue that lie, so I just grunted something neutral and changed the subject, "Hey, I wondered if you could come over? It's short notice and there's Bryan, but I wondered. Or maybe tomorrow?" I kind of winced at the begging tone in my voice, but I really missed her.

"I wish I could tonight, but Bryan is in sleep mode." She sounded regretful.

"Well, I guess we'll make it Sunday then." I was hanging on to the phone like it was the edge of a cliff. I wished I didn't have to wait four days to see her, but she had a kid and job and I didn't.

While I waited, I helped Sally get our escapees oriented. They were in shock: they had no access to their savings accounts or their relatives and they were scared of the future. We tried to help out by getting them clothes and toothbrushes, etc. Sally found a pack of cards, and it turned out that they all played bridge. Between card games and jigsaw puzzles and taking walks, they weren't completely bored.

Sally delivered meals and said the necessary words so that no one would get enthralled.

I told Sally that Taylor was coming out on Sunday, and I'd decided to tell her about fairies and everything. Sally decided to have a dinner party to celebrate.

CHAPTER THIRTY-ONE:

Sunday

I had to tell Taylor sometime.

We dropped Bryan off with Sally and Charlie and headed out for a walk in the woods. The nighttime cold was pushing the little understory plants into winter mode, leaving the ground bare, brown, and wet. The autumn forest is a harsh landscape, but one I thrive in. I inhaled great gulps of the cold, clear air like it was a cocktail. Funny how the sleeping forest makes me feel more alive.

We don't have trails in our woods, but we do have routes. I took Taylor up along the creek toward an outcrop of rocks left over from the glaciers. It's a steady climb up a long slant through the bare birches and maples and the dark green firs and pines. We sort of followed the creek—it wasn't always in sight but was always there, often hidden by tumbles of boulders. I love the rocks in the fall; the mosses dry to a brownish crust, and the yellow and orange lichens almost shine as if lit from within.

I had to go first since I knew the way, but I kept looking back, checking on Taylor. I just like to look at her, and I thought our hike might be the last one we took together.

We were well back in the woods when I heard Taylor inhale sharply, and I caught a glimpse of blue flickering between the trees down by the water. The water fairies were checking us out.

"Did you see that?" She stopped and stared off into the forest.

"Yeah," I gulped. I wasn't ready. I'd planned to tell her once we got to the outcrop near the spring.

"What was it?"

Well, maybe we were at as good a place as any. "Let's go sit by the creek," I said. I led the way, stepping from rock to rock, down a steep mossy bank to the water.

It was a lovely spot, and one I hadn't visited in a long time. There was a little waterfall, Niagara in miniature, with a stunted pine bending over it. Below the fall, a small pool was silvered with a thin layer of ice and brown and yellow with drenched leaves. I picked out a rock and sat down. Taylor found a place to perch nearby and gazed about with appreciation.

"What a lovely little place!" she sighed. "It must've been wonderful to grow up here."

"Yeah, in a lot of ways it was."

I didn't have any specific memories of that very spot; it was very familiar in the way all of our forest was familiar. I'd seen the creek in the spring when the water was an icy flow of snow melt, seen it in summer as a cool refreshing gift of life, and seen it in the winter as a frozen promise of abundance to come again.

I took a deep breath. "Taylor, I have to tell you some things about me."

She faced me, puzzled. "Deep, dark secrets?" Her smile was wary.

"Yeah." She was watching me, but I couldn't look at her. I decided to just say it, bad news first. We'd get to the good news if she stuck around.

"I killed a guy." I glanced at her. "That militia guy that

disappeared? That was me." I waited.

Then she spoke softly, tentatively, "You had a reason?"

"Not a good one. I was angry over the death of a friend."

She frowned, but with confusion. "You mean you were defending your friend?"

"Not directly. He killed a friend of mine, but he wasn't the only one responsible. I didn't have to do it." I inhaled harshly and let my breath out. "It was murder."

There was a long silence broken by a sweep of wind that rattled some branches. Far away a crow cawed, a sound that was harsh and lonely. I waited some more. The ice on the little pond wasn't white like people think ice is. It was gray in places, a silvery blue in others, and lined with crescents of black. I could see swirls of black water under the ice like blood in the veins of my wrist.

The birches weren't white either, not really. The papery bark had a creamy cast to it and browned up in horizontal lines that blackened into knots. The branches were nearly white near the tree trunk but darkened as they narrowed into spider webs of black twigs. I stared up at the twigs silhouetted against the dull blue of the late afternoon sky. A single yellow leaf detached, twirled, danced, and spiraled downward, landing at my feet.

My butt was getting sore from sitting on the rock. Taylor shifted position uncomfortably. Maybe the rocks were hard on her butt, too. Or maybe she just wasn't comfortable with me any more. But I kept waiting. I didn't want to hurry her.

Finally she spoke, her voice thin and fragile, "I don't know what to say. You don't seem like a violent guy to me."

I glanced at her face. She had her mittens up over her mouth. My throat felt tight. "I am. Or I used to be. I got in fights all the time as a kid."

"So . . . how do you feel about . . . killing that militia

guy?"

"I wish I hadn't done it."

She nodded. I looked into her sad brown eyes. She said, "I kind of wish you hadn't told me."

"Well, I had to."

"I'm kind of glad you did." She smiled but at herself for being contradictory. Taylor cleared her throat. "So . . . this is added information? I have to add this to what I know of you? I don't think I could kill someone unless that person was attacking me or Bryan, but people kill each other all the time. Like soldiers. Lots of soldiers come back from war and can't get over having killed someone."

"I saw myself as a soldier in a war." *But that's not an excuse*, I thought. So I added, "I have to find a different way to fight."

Then I stood up. "I'm going to show you my other secret." And I lifted myself up into the air above the rocks. Taylor's mouth fell open. She blinked and stuttered, "What the fuck?" I felt sort of silly just standing there in the air like a stage magician, so I flapped my arms and moved upwards. Flapping isn't necessary, it's just instinctive, I guess. Then I slid skywards toward the treetops, circled around, and flew back down toward the creek. I ended up hovering in the air in front of Taylor. I couldn't help grinning. It was embarrassing showing off like that. She jumped to her feet and clapped her hands over her mouth.

"Look, I know this is hard to believe, but I'm not altogether human," I told her.

"My god, you're standing in the air!"

"Yeah," I shrugged. I dropped down to the rocks and climbed back up to my original perch. "Sit down, Taylor. I'll try to explain."

"That was fucking wonderful!" She didn't sit down.

"How do you do that?"

I shrugged again. "Okay, here's the thing. The nature spirits the Native Americans believed in back in the old days? We're real. I mean not exactly the way their stories were, but basically they were right. We do exist. There's a whole family of water fairies that live in a spring upstream from here. I'm more a forest fairy."

Her mouth was a round "O". "What . . . what about Charlie and Sally? Hey, is Arne like a troll or something?"

I had to laugh. "Sally's a raven, but Charlie and Arne are just people."

"Oh, my God, even more information!" She wrapped her arms around her head and kind of scrunched up her face. I laughed again. "So you can't grant wishes or anything like that? That would be just too much. I can't believe that."

"Well, you're right. I can't. I can kind of hypnotize people a little bit, and I can do some weird things with time . . ."

"Bryan!" she shouted. "That's why he gets quiet around you!"

"Well, yeah, sometimes." I shrugged an apology. "Just every now and then."

"Oh, my God." She rubbed her face with her hands. Then she really surprised me, asking, "Can you teach me to fly?"

"No. I wish I could," I told her. "But I think I can carry you with me." Taylor is a lot shorter than me, so I had to bend down. I bear-hugged her with my arms under her armpits, and she eagerly wrapped her arms around my neck. Then I headed upwards, slowly because she was at least one-thirty, I'd bet. We got about the height of the treetops when she nearly deafened me with her yell of delight; her mouth was right by my ear. "Oh, my God, this is so beautiful!"

She was seeing our forest from the air for the first

time, a view I take a little too much for granted. I couldn't concentrate on the view, though. She'd wrapped her legs around my waist, and even through her sweater and jeans, I was getting ideas . . . *Stop that*, I told myself. *But I bet it would be totally awesome to try it on a warm night. Under the stars.*

I needed to concentrate on holding Taylor up; she was sagging, pulling on my neck and back. I revolved in a slow circle to give her a view all around, but I was sinking; the extra weight was a real drag on my energy as well as my bones and muscles. In fact, I could feel her slipping.

"Hey, my arms are getting tired." She had a death grip around my neck. My arms were tiring too. "Okay," I said, "Down we go."

"This is amazing. Just amazing." Her clinging to me was amazing too. I dropped us slowly down between the pines and birches to the edge of the stream. The landing was clumsy; my feet hit the rocks and I stumbled and almost dropped her, but we managed to get on the ground without falling on our butts. Taylor's cheeks were red with cold, and her eyes lit like stars. I wanted to hug her again, but wasn't sure if it would be welcome without the flying. So I just said, "Yeah, I like to fly."

"Oh, boy, is it ever amazing!"

Then a pause opened up between us that was definitely awkward. We couldn't keep batting comments about flying back and forth forever. We stopped looking at each other, and Taylor fiddled with a strand of her hair. Then she said, "Bobby, you've overloaded me with information. Do you get that?"

I said, "Yeah, I do. Let's go back then. Do you still feel like staying for the party?"

She hugged herself and gazed around at the woods. "You

know, I could always tell this place was magic somehow. I just didn't know magic was real. Yes, I'd like to stay for the party."

CHAPTER THIRTY TWO:

Later that Day

When Sally throws a party, she goes all out. She called the water fairies, too. Yeah, they have a cell phone. They keep it in a plastic box wedged into the rocks somewhere. Anyway, they came down for the evening. She'd given the Minnesota coyotes an invite, too, but they didn't feel like making the trip.

The refugees came out of fairy time to join in, dressed in regular clothes from the second hand shop—no more jailhouse orange, except for Mr. Moore, who wore his shirt like a badge of honor. The ladies looked a little rough without their perms and make up, but there wasn't much we could do about that. Arne came to the party too, looking rough himself because he'd fallen off the wagon again.

Sally cooked up a huge repast with Charlie as second-in-command: a leafy salad with carrots and nuts and cabbage and all kinds of good stuff in it, a side of sweet potatoes coated with brown sugar, green beans, trout sautéed in wine for the carnivores, cornbread, and lots and lots of pies.

Most of the mob had already shown up when Taylor and I got back from our walk. Bryan was in a tizzy from all the excitement, so I just had time for a quick hug before he broke loose and ran into the kitchen. Charlie caught him in a bear hug and gave him a wooden spoon and a bowl to play with. Taylor and I stood in the doorway and watched the swirl of activity.

Sally yelled, "Eat, drink, with no obligation!" out the kitchen door before Charlie handed out the first drinks. I got Taylor a glass of hot cider and we toasted each other. She was grinning, enjoying the noise and confusion. I said, "Let's walk around, and I'll introduce you to everyone." So we made a circuit, exchanging names and greetings. Taylor was stunned—for the third time that day—when she found out that we were hiding the jail escapees. But she handled it by peeling off to help Sally get the food into serving dishes.

We didn't have room for everyone around the table, so folks were all over Sally's cabin: perched on the couch, the chairs, sitting on the floor, wherever. Taylor, Sally, and Charlie handed out the food and the second round of alcohol. We decided to toast the return of cold weather with hot rum toddies. I overheard Mrs. Moore asking the Muslim gal—Puteri Munsi is her name—if she could drink, and she said, "I'm not a strict Muslim." Bryan banged his drum through the first course and danced through the second and third.

Of course, everyone had to tell their stories. Puteri had been a college professor, was a poet, and had gone into hiding when her brother and his family got rounded up. She was from Malaysia. That is, her parents were. She was born in Minneapolis.

I asked Taylor if she knew what story the militia had spread about the great escape. "Officially?" she asked. "The newspaper says that someone tasered the militia guy and made him let everyone out the back door. But there's gossip that says different."

"I wanna hear the gossip."

"Well, one story is that the militia guy claimed that everyone just vanished. Just vanished like with magic."

There was general laughter at that. Taylor blushed. "Was it magic?" she asked.

"Yep." We all told her the story together, so it came out really confusing with Mrs. Moore talking about angels, Mrs. Allen talking about not taking things too literally, and me talking about coyotes and fairy time. I could tell that she was drowning again, but she was able to get the gist of it all.

We went on to drink more and more, and Sally got some blunts started so the room filled up with smoke, and finally we all reached that point where everyone got kind of philosophical and started talking about God and Allah and spirits.

Mrs. Allen started hunting through her Bible to find references to nature and recited, "I lift my eyes to the hills from whence cometh my help."

Puteri came back at her with a quote from the Qu'ran: "There is not an animal that lives on the earth, nor a being that flies on its wings, but they form communities like you. Nothing have we omitted from the Book, and they all shall be gathered to their Lord in the end."

Sally got on her high horse about Deep Ecology—she has a BS from a university in Washington. And Charlie started reciting poetry.

After awhile—between the smoke, the wood stove, and all the warm bodies—we got hot, so we migrated outside and built a bonfire. At some point, Sally and the water fairies decided to demonstrate a flying fairy dance, and that pretty much topped the evening. I didn't join them in the air because I didn't want to leave Taylor. It was weird to watch from the ground; I kind of got the human perspective. They—Sally and the fairies—looked wild and beautiful up against the night sky and the stars, lit from below by the fire.

I could tell that Taylor was overwhelmed again.

After that people started drifting off, saying good night and goodbye, and the party dwindled down to me, Taylor, Arne, Sally, and Charlie, with Bryan zonked out on the couch. When Taylor fell asleep in the armchair, I said my last goodbyes and walked home to my cabin.

CHAPTER THIRTY THREE:

Late December

So that's how it all went down, the summer of fighting and change.

Sally's kitchen is a cozy Santa's workshop now: ticky-tacky with Christmas arts and crafts, steeped in the scents of tea and honey, and sugar-saturated with seasonal baking.

She's preparing for the solstice, but it looks more like a Christmas party. Mrs. Moore is a real traditionalist and, since she couldn't get anyone else interested in popcorn chains, she sat herself down at Sally's kitchen table and strung them all herself. She made Christmas trees from construction paper and decorated them with red, yellow, and blue cut out ornaments too. I told her I wasn't cutting down any trees for her to decorate, so she'd have to make do.

We'll be celebrating the turn of the solstice with another dance. Sally is planning even more of a drunken blow-out than the last one, which should be interesting. The water fairies are coming for sure, and they've put the word out all over, so we're expecting some from clear over in North Dakota where the fracking has ruined the lakes.

The fairies need somewhere to go, so they're going to stop at our place on their way to Ontario or Saskatchewan.

The coyotes are coming too.

Our resort is full, though you'd have to be a fairy to know it. We still haven't figured out how to get our refugees to Canada. I don't think the trip itself would be hard, but the problem is getting them motivated to leave. They spend all their time taking walks and playing cards and, now that they've all phoned their relatives using burner phones, they're happy enough and not in any hurry to go.

Except Puteri. She's gone off with some coyotes to set up a route for a new underground railroad. Yeah, we've agreed to be a waystation if she finds more people in need of help. Mrs. Allen says that we'll be honored by history like the other Underground Railroad, and the memory of our actions will live on even if no one ever knows our names. I told her that we sure as hell didn't need to get famous, but I got her point about doing the right thing.

Taylor and Bryan come out to visit every weekend. I take Bryan up in the air now, he loves to fly. Taylor likes to hang out in the kitchen or on the porch, letting life swirl around her: the scents of Sally's cooking, Charlie's chatting about this and that, the dogs playing, and the refugees milling about—always underfoot, it seems to me.

Sally keeps thrusting food at Taylor, but Taylor understands about enthralling, so she always waits for me to say the words. We're just friends . . . well, on the surface, anyway, we're just friends. But I live in hope.

I go out to visit the Congressman and the Russians every week or so. Mrs. Allen says I'm a missionary visiting the cannibals. I told them that I'll bring them back to real time if they ever get their values right, but so far they haven't progressed beyond yelling at each other and me. In fact, I left about three seconds after I arrived last time because one of the Russians had a gun aimed at me. But I will keep working on befriending them.

Because you have to fight back some way, don't you? That's my only comfort—besides good friends and family, I mean. You have to fight back to have any self-respect. Even if you're going to lose, you have to know you tried. But the trick, like Mrs. Allen says, is to not become like the enemies yourself.

So I'm fighting like a wild hare: smart, sneaky, dodging this way and that, a moving target, but leaving the violence behind. I'll screw the militia whenever I can. I'll help the refugees. I'll exile the next fucking Congressman that comes up here. And I'll keep fighting until I die and become one with the stars.

Like my momma always said: feed, fuck, and *fight*.

Thank you for taking the time
to read *Wild Hare*.

COULD YOU TAKE A MOMENT TO GIVE THE BOOK
A SHORT REVIEW ON AMAZON.COM? YOUR REVIEWS
MEAN THE WORLD TO OUR AUTHORS, AND HELP
STORIES SUCH AS THIS ONE REACH A WIDER
AUDIENCE. THANK YOU SO MUCH!

Find links to
Wild Hare
AND ALL OUR GREAT BOOKS
ON AMAZON OR AT WWW.WHOCHAINSYOU.COM.

AUTHOR

Acknowledgments

Thank you to my publisher, Tamira. Without her, I would not be a published author.

Author

Laura Koerber is an artist and writer who lives on an island with her husband and two dogs. Laura divides her retirement time between dog rescue, care for disabled people, political activism, and yes, she tells herself stories while driving.

Her first book, *The Dog Thief and Other Stories* (written as Jill Kearney), was listed by Kirkus Review as one of the Hundred Best Indie Books of 2015. She's also the author of *The Listener's Tale, I Once Was Lost, But Now I'm Found, Limbo, The Shapeshifter's Tale, The Eclipse Dancer,* and *Wild Hare.*

Also from Laura Koerber

The Eclipse Dancer

Andy thought of flying. She imagined the air under her arms, her hair lifting and floating. She felt her heart-beat separate from the faraway beat and form its own rhythm: light, quick, a dancing thrum. When she opened her eyes, her yard was dusky and her mood had lightened.

She let her gaze drift across the darkening landscape. Andy's heart filled with exultation. She raised her arms, fanned out her fingers, and arched her feet until she was on her toes.

She was assaulted by memories. Her mother was dying, and Danny had been dead for years. Her daughter was in Minneapolis, and Alana was up in the North Woods someplace. All of her childhood friends—the fairies, Hairy, Mr. Tolliver, and Kenshi—were gone.

Is it true that childhood is never overcome? "I have changed," she whispered.

She gently rose up into the warm, dark air and began to dance. *Read more and order from whochainsyou.com, Amazon, and other outlets.*

Also from Laura Koerber

LIMBO

How would you spend your time if you died and found yourself in Limbo? Most see Purgatory as a kind of in-between afterlife for people who didn't rate Heaven and don't deserve Hell. The author's Limbo is a ghost town that includes animals that had been killed by humans: a dog, some cats, cows, chickens, and wild creatures, too. The animals are content with their lot in the afterlife, but the humans have an infinity of time on their hands and not enough to do. They think about the big issues, of course: the nature of God, how they screwed up in life, and how they can escape Limbo and get into Heaven.

But no one can spend all their time thinking higher thoughts, so mostly they do what they did in life: they gossip, they get on each other's nerves, and they play poker.

If you like Ghost-Lite stories, you'll love Limbo...you'll laugh, cry, and ponder what comes next in the great beyond.

Read more and order from whochainsyou.com, Amazon, and other outlets.

Also from Laura Koerber

THE DOG THIEF AND OTHER STORIES
WRITING AS JILL KEARNEY

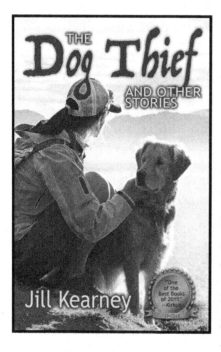

"**D**ecrepit humans rescue desperate canines, cats and the occasional rat in this collection of shaggy but piercing short stories."

Listed by Kirkus Review as one of the best books of 2015, this collection of short stories and a novella explores the complexity of relationships between people and animals in an impoverished rural community where the connections people have with animals are sometimes their only connection to life.

According to Kirkus Review: "Kearney treats her characters, and their relationships with their pets, with a cleareyed, unsentimental sensitivity and psychological depth. Through their struggles, she shows readers a search for meaning through the humblest acts of caretaking and companionship. A superb collection of stories about the most elemental of bonds."

Read more and order from whochainsyou.com, Amazon, and other outlets.

About who chains you Books

WELCOME TO WHO CHAINS YOU: BOOKS FOR THOSE WHO BELIEVE PEOPLE—AND ANIMALS—DESERVE TO BE FREE.

At Who Chains You Books our mission is a simple one—to amplify the voices of the animals through the empowerment of animal lovers, activists, and rescuers to write and publish books elevating the status of animals in today's society.

We hope you'll visit our website and join us on this adventure we call animal advocacy publishing. We welcome you.

Read more about us at whochainsyou.com.

Made in the USA
Monee, IL
07 December 2019

18133107R00105